S0-ARG-230

BILLY BATSON AND THE MAGIC OF SHAZAM!

STONE ARCH BOOKS
a capstone imprint

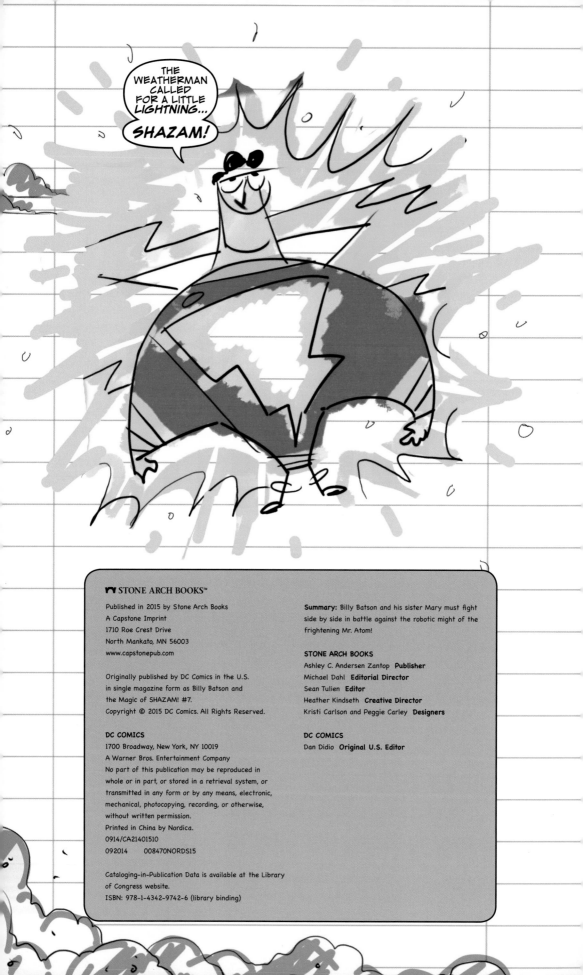

STONE ARCH BOOKS™

Published in 2015 by Stone Arch Books
A Capstone Imprint
1710 Roe Crest Drive
North Mankato, MN 56003
www.capstonepub.com

Originally published by DC Comics in the U.S.
in single magazine form as Billy Batson and
the Magic of SHAZAM! #7.
Copyright © 2015 DC Comics. All Rights Reserved.

DC COMICS
1700 Broadway, New York, NY 10019
A Warner Bros. Entertainment Company
No part of this publication may be reproduced in
whole or in part, or stored in a retrieval system, or
transmitted in any form or by any means, electronic,
mechanical, photocopying, recording, or otherwise,
without written permission.
Printed in China by Nordica.
0914/CA21401510
092014   008470NORDS15

Cataloging-in-Publication Data is available at the Library
of Congress website.
ISBN: 978-1-4342-9742-6 (library binding)

Summary: Billy Batson and his sister Mary must fight
side by side in battle against the robotic might of the
frightening Mr. Atom!

STONE ARCH BOOKS

Ashley C. Andersen Zantop **Publisher**
Michael Dahl **Editorial Director**
Sean Tulien **Editor**
Heather Kindseth **Creative Director**
Kristi Carlson and Peggie Carley **Designers**

DC COMICS
Dan Didio **Original U.S. Editor**

BILLY BATSON AND THE MAGIC OF SHAZAM!

Deception Reception!

Art Baltazar & Franco ....writers
Byron Vaughns..........................illustrator
Dave Tanguay.............................colorist

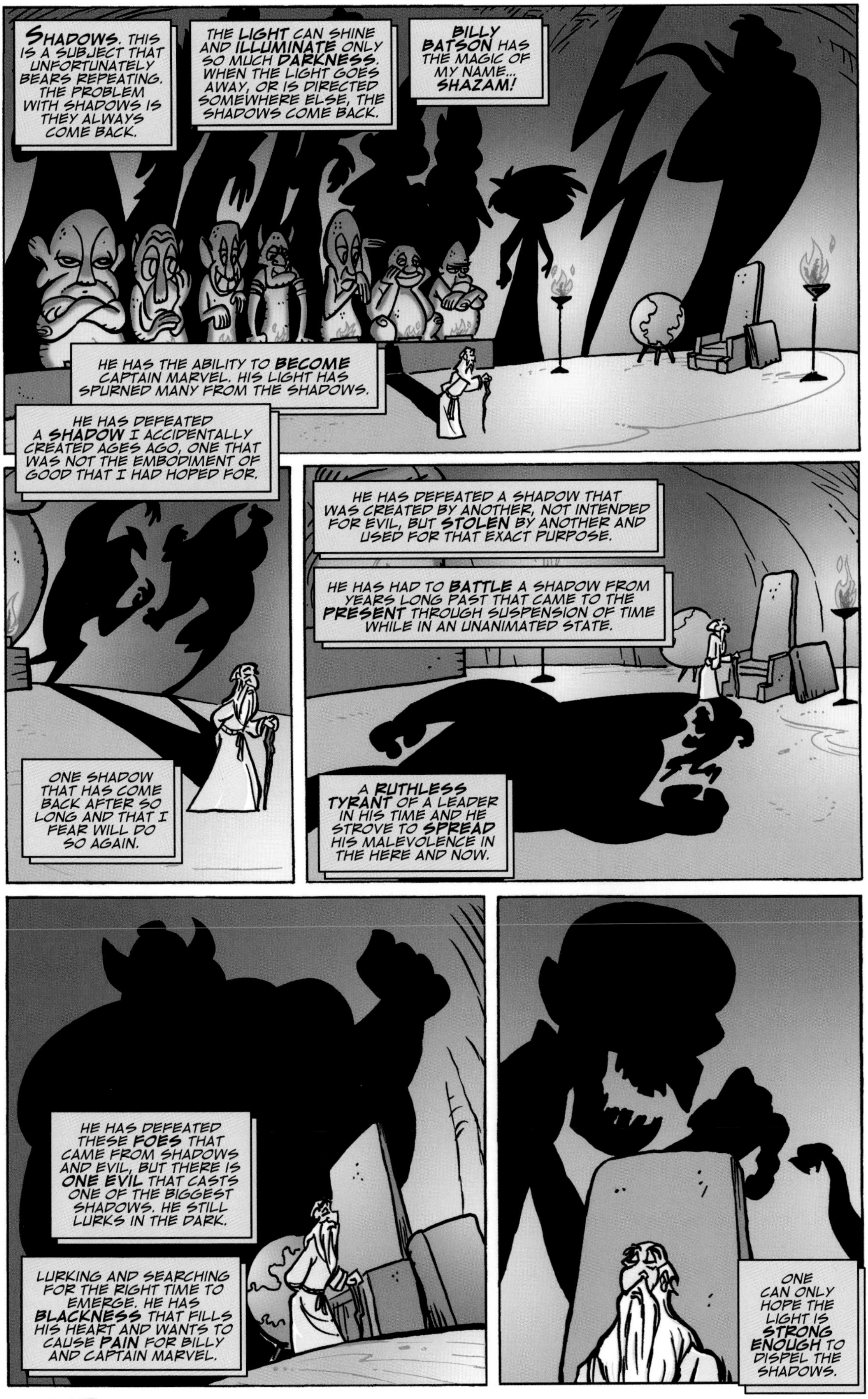
SHADOWS. THIS IS A SUBJECT THAT UNFORTUNATELY BEARS REPEATING. THE PROBLEM WITH SHADOWS IS THEY ALWAYS COME BACK.
THE LIGHT CAN SHINE AND ILLUMINATE ONLY SO MUCH DARKNESS. WHEN THE LIGHT GOES AWAY, OR IS DIRECTED SOMEWHERE ELSE, THE SHADOWS COME BACK.
BILLY BATSON HAS THE MAGIC OF MY NAME... SHAZAM!
HE HAS THE ABILITY TO BECOME CAPTAIN MARVEL. HIS LIGHT HAS SPURNED MANY FROM THE SHADOWS.
HE HAS DEFEATED A SHADOW I ACCIDENTALLY CREATED AGES AGO, ONE THAT WAS NOT THE EMBODIMENT OF GOOD THAT I HAD HOPED FOR.
ONE SHADOW THAT HAS COME BACK AFTER SO LONG AND THAT I FEAR WILL DO SO AGAIN.
HE HAS DEFEATED A SHADOW THAT WAS CREATED BY ANOTHER, NOT INTENDED FOR EVIL, BUT STOLEN BY ANOTHER AND USED FOR THAT EXACT PURPOSE.
HE HAS HAD TO BATTLE A SHADOW FROM YEARS LONG PAST THAT CAME TO THE PRESENT THROUGH SUSPENSION OF TIME WHILE IN AN UNANIMATED STATE.
A RUTHLESS TYRANT OF A LEADER IN HIS TIME AND HE STROVE TO SPREAD HIS MALEVOLENCE IN THE HERE AND NOW.
HE HAS DEFEATED THESE FOES THAT CAME FROM SHADOWS AND EVIL, BUT THERE IS ONE EVIL THAT CASTS ONE OF THE BIGGEST SHADOWS. HE STILL LURKS IN THE DARK.
LURKING AND SEARCHING FOR THE RIGHT TIME TO EMERGE. HE HAS BLACKNESS THAT FILLS HIS HEART AND WANTS TO CAUSE PAIN FOR BILLY AND CAPTAIN MARVEL.
ONE CAN ONLY HOPE THE LIGHT IS STRONG ENOUGH TO DISPEL THE SHADOWS.

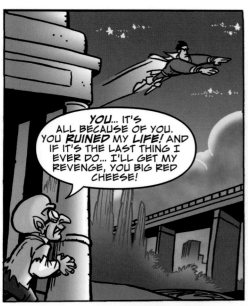

YOU... IT'S ALL BECAUSE OF YOU. YOU *RUINED* MY *LIFE!* AND IF IT'S THE LAST THING I EVER DO... I'LL GET MY REVENGE, YOU BIG RED CHEESE!

HEY *DOC!* HOW COME WE GOTTA SLEEP OUT HERE WHEN WE GOT A PERFECTLY GOOD WARM PLACE TO SLEEP?

NOT TO MENTION THE *OTHER* PLACE WE HAVE TOO.

YEAH! WE GOT *TWO PLACES* WE CAN STAY, YET WE'RE OUT HERE IN THE *COLD!*

I'VE *EXPLAINED* THIS TO YOU BEFORE. YOU--

EVENING JOE, BILL, DOC... HOW YOU BOYS BEEN? HAVEN'T SEEN YOU IN A WHILE. THOUGHT MAYBE SOMETHING HAD *HAPPENED* TO YOU.

ME AND A COUPLE OF THE OTHER GUYS WERE GOING TO COME LOOK FOR YOU TOMORROW.

OH! HEH HEH...NO NEED FOR THAT, YOU KNOW HOW THE *VAGRANT LIFE* CAN BE, WANDERING AIMLESSLY FROM PLACE TO PLACE...

HEH HEH. NO, NO TROUBLE HERE, JUST LIVING THE LIFESTYLE OF THE *BROKE* AND *HOMELESS*...

YES... WELL... GLAD TO SEE YOU BOYS ARE OK.

HAVE A *GOOD NIGHT!*

HOW MANY TIMES DO I HAVE TO *EXPLAIN* THIS? THAT IS *EXACTLY* WHY WE HAVE TO SLEEP OUT HERE. BECAUSE PEOPLE WILL WONDER WHERE WE'VE BEEN.

WE DO NOT WANT TO *ATTRACT* ANY *ATTENTION* TO THE WAREHOUSE OR THE BUILDING WHERE WE BROUGHT THAT *KULL STATUE.* EVERY ONCE IN A WHILE, FOR THE FORESEEABLE FUTURE, WE NEED TO PRETEND LIKE WE ARE STILL *HOMELESS*, SO SHUT UP AND GO TO SLEEP NOW!

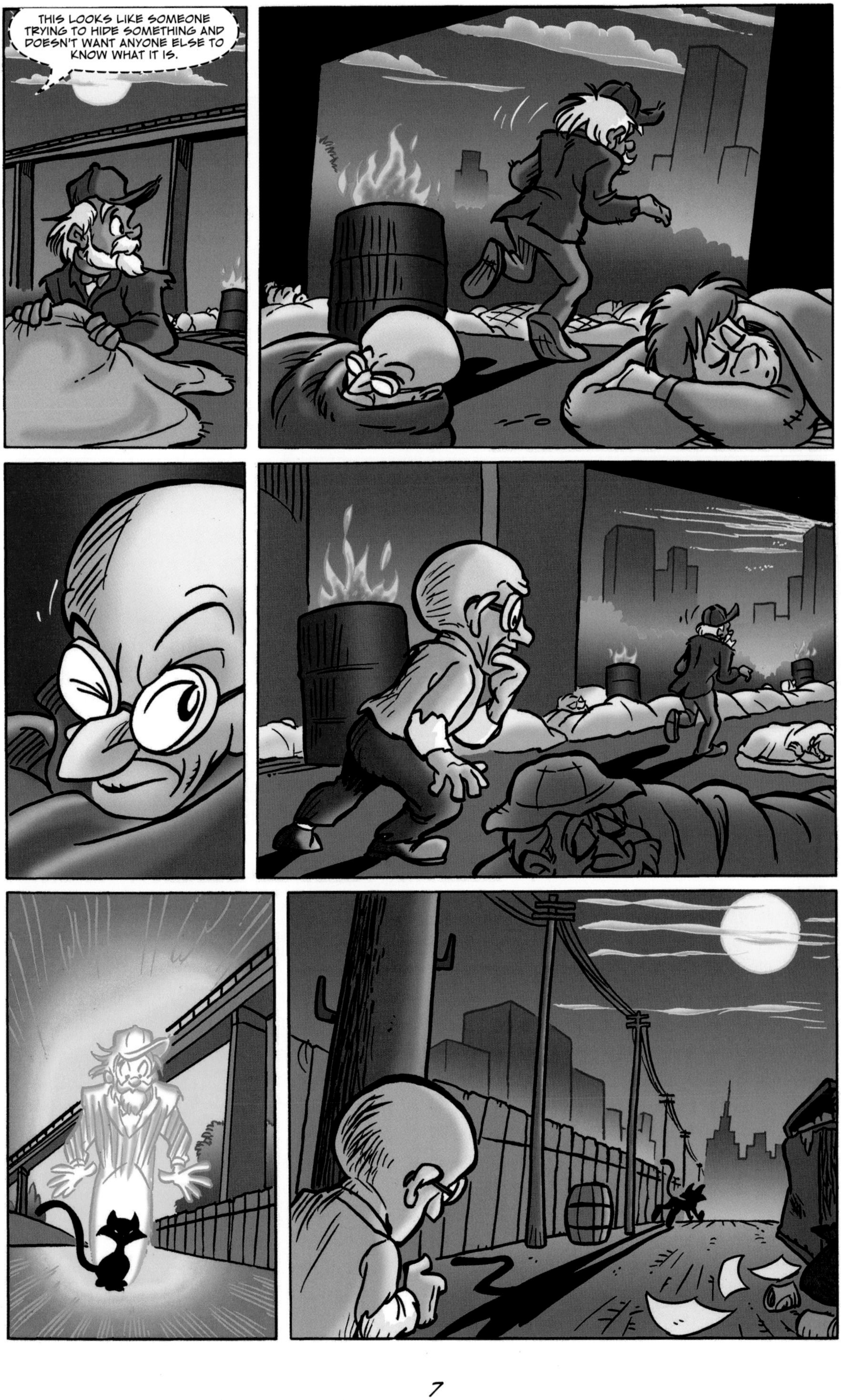
THIS LOOKS LIKE SOMEONE TRYING TO HIDE SOMETHING AND DOESN'T WANT ANYONE ELSE TO KNOW WHAT IT IS.

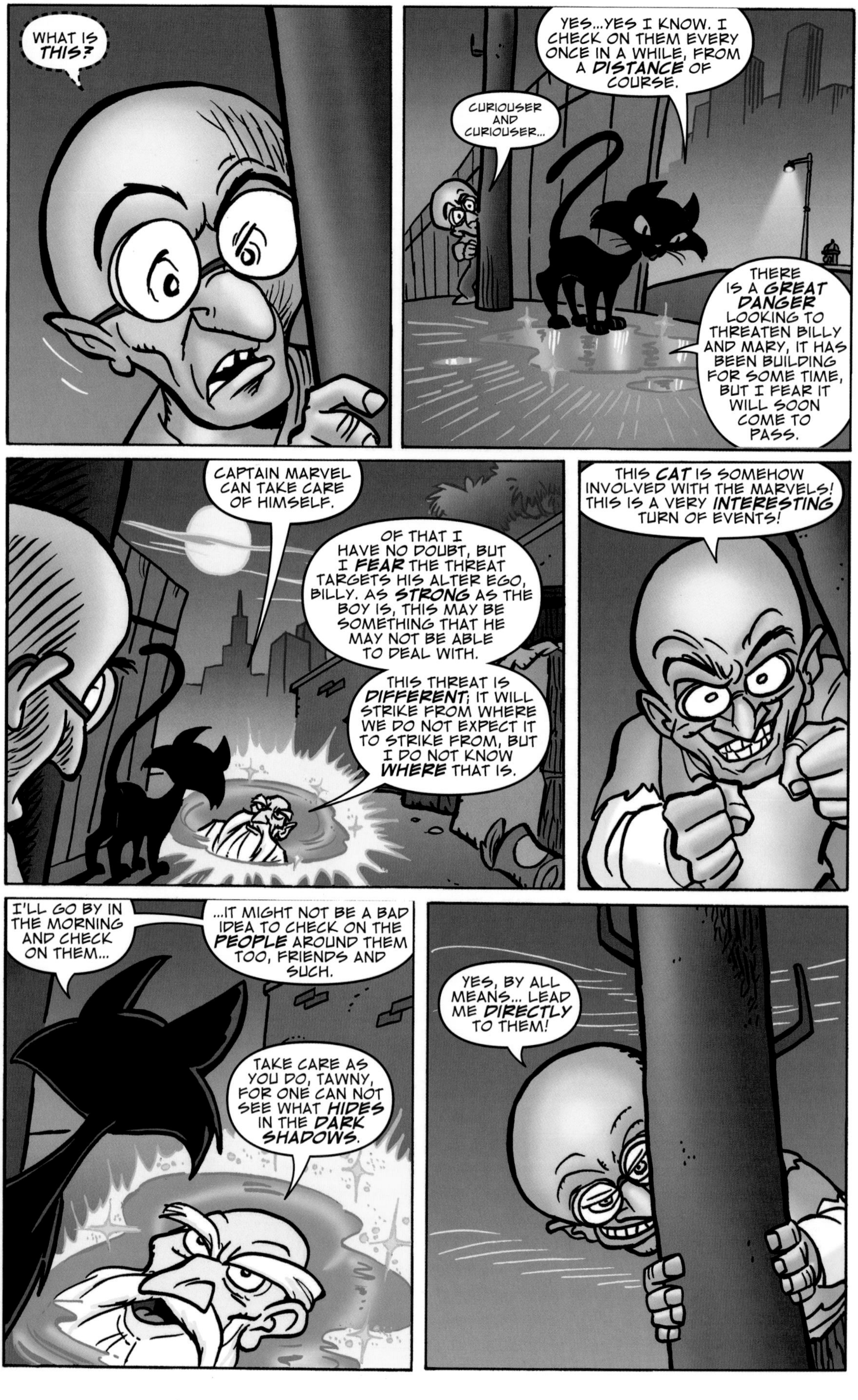

WHAT IS THIS?
YES...YES I KNOW. I CHECK ON THEM EVERY ONCE IN A WHILE, FROM A DISTANCE OF COURSE.
CURIOUSER AND CURIOUSER...
THERE IS A GREAT DANGER LOOKING TO THREATEN BILLY AND MARY, IT HAS BEEN BUILDING FOR SOME TIME, BUT I FEAR IT WILL SOON COME TO PASS.
CAPTAIN MARVEL CAN TAKE CARE OF HIMSELF.
OF THAT I HAVE NO DOUBT, BUT I FEAR THE THREAT TARGETS HIS ALTER EGO, BILLY. AS STRONG AS THE BOY IS, THIS MAY BE SOMETHING THAT HE MAY NOT BE ABLE TO DEAL WITH.
THIS THREAT IS DIFFERENT; IT WILL STRIKE FROM WHERE WE DO NOT EXPECT IT TO STRIKE FROM, BUT I DO NOT KNOW WHERE THAT IS.
THIS CAT IS SOMEHOW INVOLVED WITH THE MARVELS! THIS IS A VERY INTERESTING TURN OF EVENTS!
I'LL GO BY IN THE MORNING AND CHECK ON THEM...
...IT MIGHT NOT BE A BAD IDEA TO CHECK ON THE PEOPLE AROUND THEM TOO, FRIENDS AND SUCH.
TAKE CARE AS YOU DO, TAWNY, FOR ONE CAN NOT SEE WHAT HIDES IN THE DARK SHADOWS.
YES, BY ALL MEANS... LEAD ME DIRECTLY TO THEM!

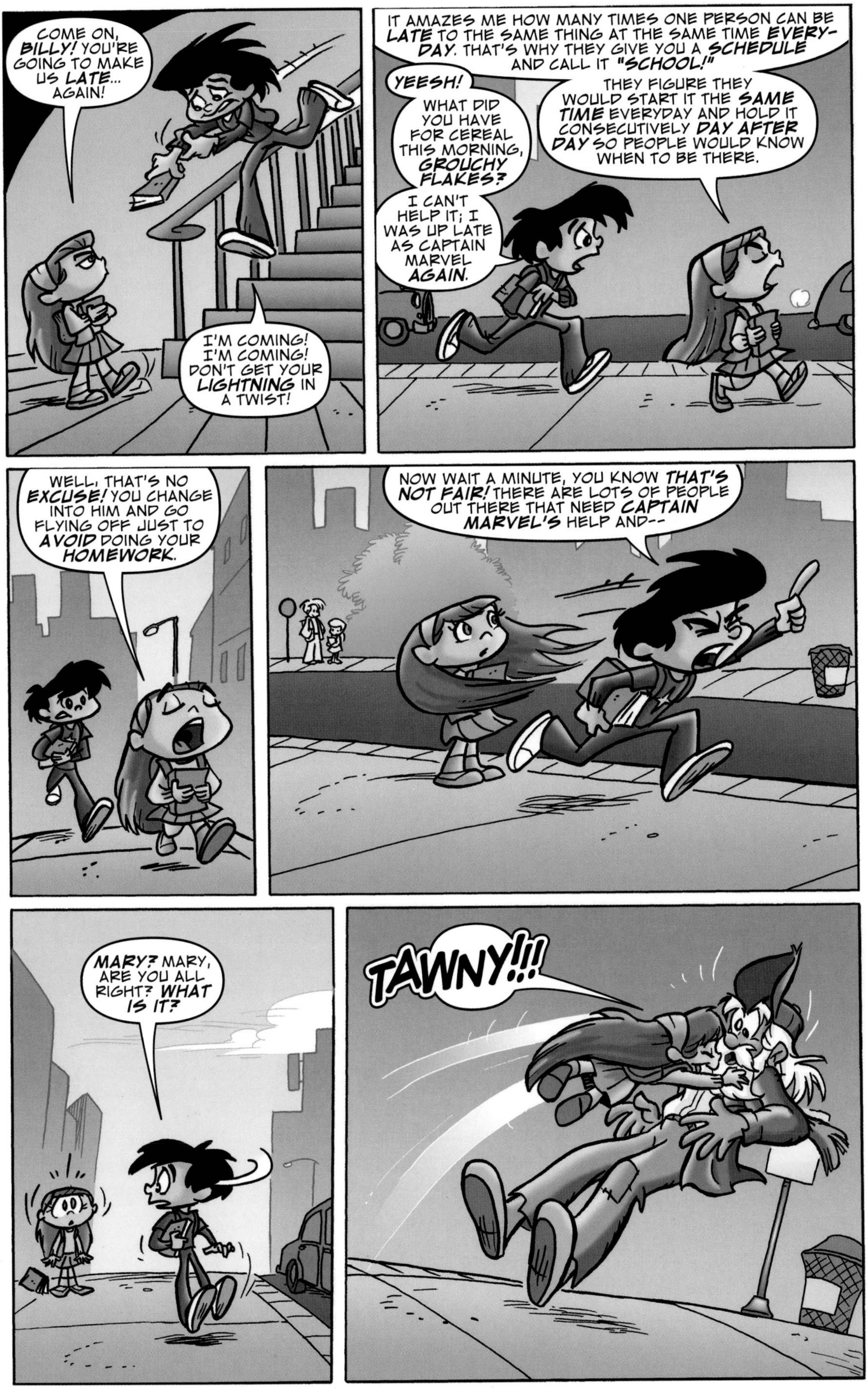
COME ON, BILLY! YOU'RE GOING TO MAKE US LATE... AGAIN!
I'M COMING! I'M COMING! DON'T GET YOUR LIGHTNING IN A TWIST!
IT AMAZES ME HOW MANY TIMES ONE PERSON CAN BE LATE TO THE SAME THING AT THE SAME TIME EVERY-DAY. THAT'S WHY THEY GIVE YOU A SCHEDULE AND CALL IT "SCHOOL!"
THEY FIGURE THEY WOULD START IT THE SAME TIME EVERYDAY AND HOLD IT CONSECUTIVELY DAY AFTER DAY SO PEOPLE WOULD KNOW WHEN TO BE THERE.
YEESH!
WHAT DID YOU HAVE FOR CEREAL THIS MORNING, GROUCHY FLAKES?
I CAN'T HELP IT; I WAS UP LATE AS CAPTAIN MARVEL AGAIN.
WELL, THAT'S NO EXCUSE! YOU CHANGE INTO HIM AND GO FLYING OFF JUST TO AVOID DOING YOUR HOMEWORK.
NOW WAIT A MINUTE, YOU KNOW THAT'S NOT FAIR! THERE ARE LOTS OF PEOPLE OUT THERE THAT NEED CAPTAIN MARVEL'S HELP AND--
MARY? MARY, ARE YOU ALL RIGHT? WHAT IS IT?
TAWNY!!!

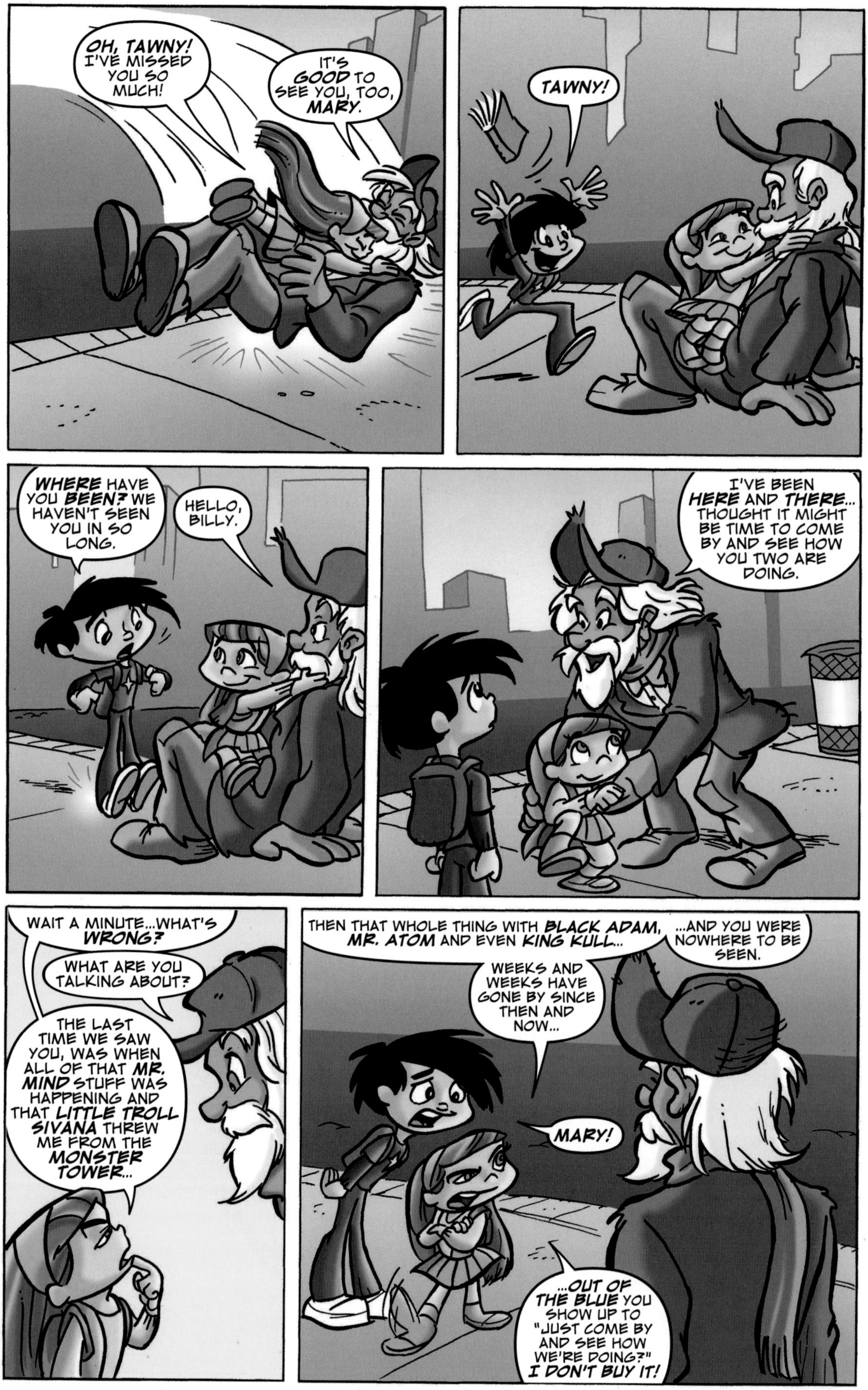
OH, TAWNY! I'VE MISSED YOU SO MUCH!
IT'S GOOD TO SEE YOU, TOO, MARY.
TAWNY!
WHERE HAVE YOU BEEN? WE HAVEN'T SEEN YOU IN SO LONG.
HELLO, BILLY.
I'VE BEEN HERE AND THERE... THOUGHT IT MIGHT BE TIME TO COME BY AND SEE HOW YOU TWO ARE DOING.
WAIT A MINUTE...WHAT'S WRONG?
WHAT ARE YOU TALKING ABOUT?
THE LAST TIME WE SAW YOU, WAS WHEN ALL OF THAT MR. MIND STUFF WAS HAPPENING AND THAT LITTLE TROLL SIVANA THREW ME FROM THE MONSTER TOWER...
THEN THAT WHOLE THING WITH BLACK ADAM, MR. ATOM AND EVEN KING KULL...
...AND YOU WERE NOWHERE TO BE SEEN.
WEEKS AND WEEKS HAVE GONE BY SINCE THEN AND NOW...
MARY!
...OUT OF THE BLUE YOU SHOW UP TO "JUST COME BY AND SEE HOW WE'RE DOING?" I DON'T BUY IT!

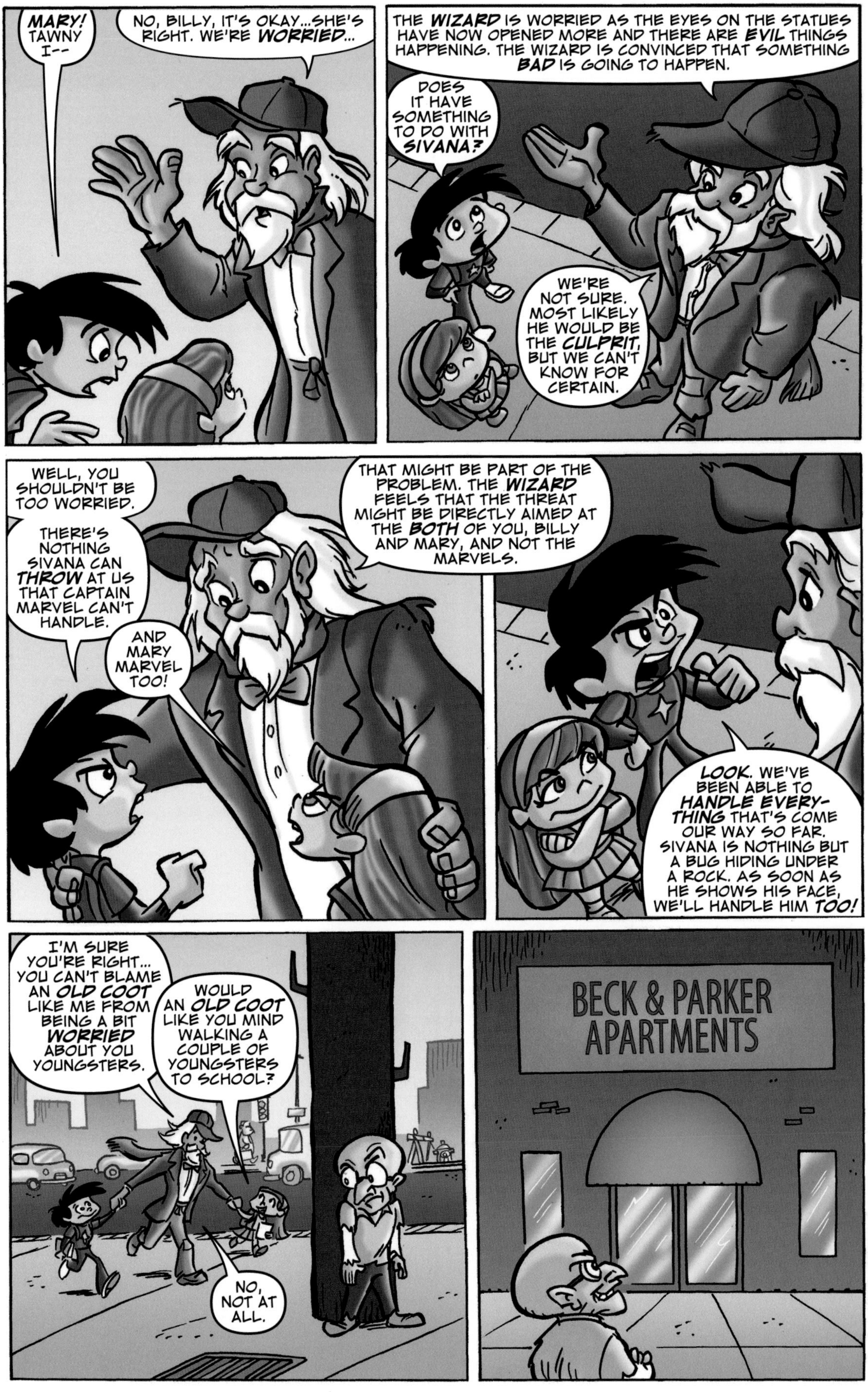

MARY! TAWNY I--
NO, BILLY, IT'S OKAY...SHE'S RIGHT. WE'RE WORRIED...
THE WIZARD IS WORRIED AS THE EYES ON THE STATUES HAVE NOW OPENED MORE AND THERE ARE EVIL THINGS HAPPENING. THE WIZARD IS CONVINCED THAT SOMETHING BAD IS GOING TO HAPPEN.
DOES IT HAVE SOMETHING TO DO WITH SIVANA?
WE'RE NOT SURE. MOST LIKELY HE WOULD BE THE CULPRIT, BUT WE CAN'T KNOW FOR CERTAIN.
WELL, YOU SHOULDN'T BE TOO WORRIED.
THERE'S NOTHING SIVANA CAN THROW AT US THAT CAPTAIN MARVEL CAN'T HANDLE.
AND MARY MARVEL TOO!
THAT MIGHT BE PART OF THE PROBLEM. THE WIZARD FEELS THAT THE THREAT MIGHT BE DIRECTLY AIMED AT THE BOTH OF YOU, BILLY AND MARY, AND NOT THE MARVELS.
LOOK. WE'VE BEEN ABLE TO HANDLE EVERY-THING THAT'S COME OUR WAY SO FAR. SIVANA IS NOTHING BUT A BUG HIDING UNDER A ROCK. AS SOON AS HE SHOWS HIS FACE, WE'LL HANDLE HIM TOO!
I'M SURE YOU'RE RIGHT... YOU CAN'T BLAME AN OLD COOT LIKE ME FROM BEING A BIT WORRIED ABOUT YOU YOUNGSTERS.
WOULD AN OLD COOT LIKE YOU MIND WALKING A COUPLE OF YOUNGSTERS TO SCHOOL?
NO, NOT AT ALL.
BECK & PARKER APARTMENTS

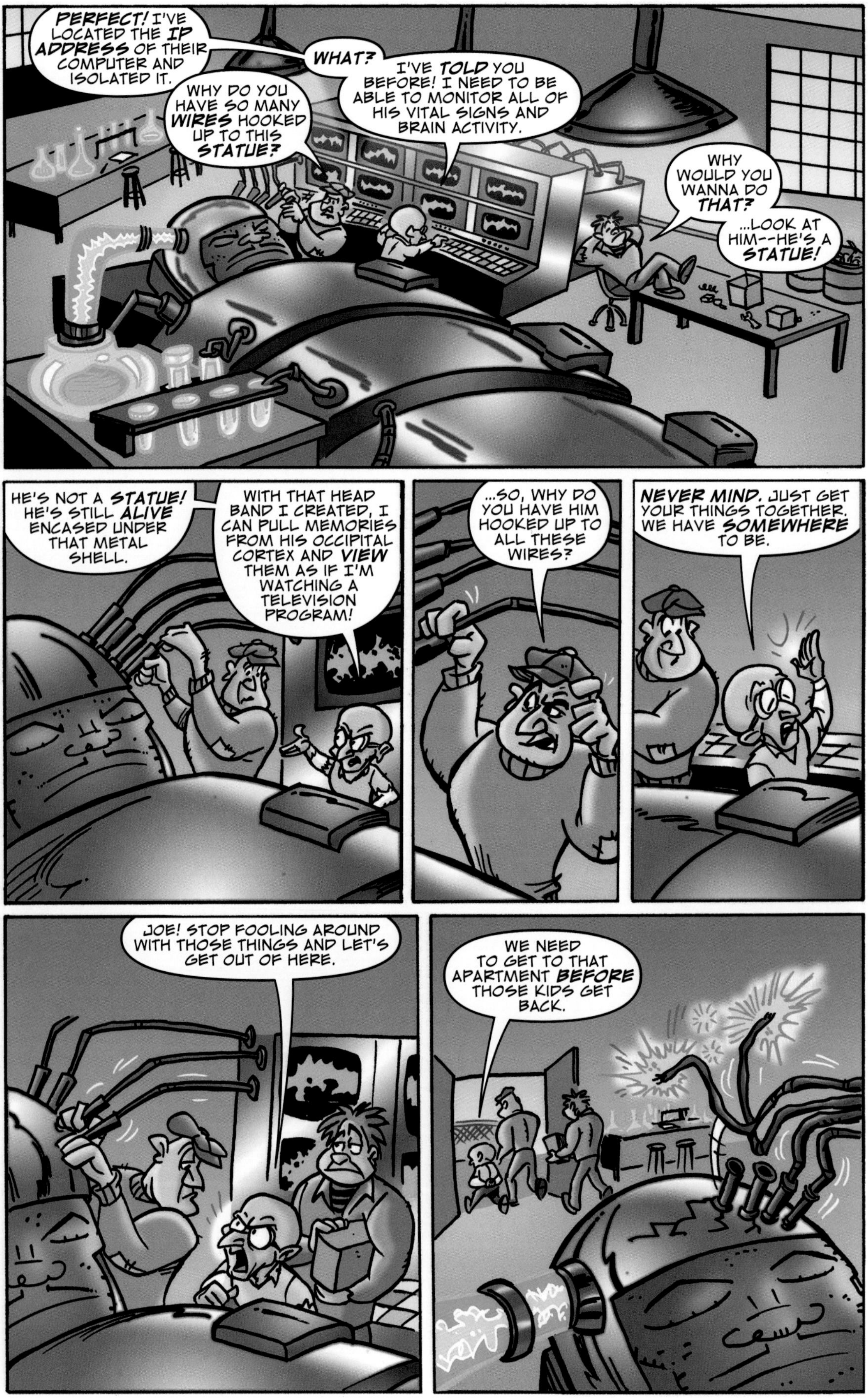
PERFECT! I'VE LOCATED THE IP ADDRESS OF THEIR COMPUTER AND ISOLATED IT.
WHAT?
WHY DO YOU HAVE SO MANY WIRES HOOKED UP TO THIS STATUE?
I'VE TOLD YOU BEFORE! I NEED TO BE ABLE TO MONITOR ALL OF HIS VITAL SIGNS AND BRAIN ACTIVITY.
WHY WOULD YOU WANNA DO THAT?
...LOOK AT HIM--HE'S A STATUE!
HE'S NOT A STATUE! HE'S STILL ALIVE ENCASED UNDER THAT METAL SHELL.
WITH THAT HEAD BAND I CREATED, I CAN PULL MEMORIES FROM HIS OCCIPITAL CORTEX AND VIEW THEM AS IF I'M WATCHING A TELEVISION PROGRAM!
...SO, WHY DO YOU HAVE HIM HOOKED UP TO ALL THESE WIRES?
NEVER MIND. JUST GET YOUR THINGS TOGETHER. WE HAVE SOMEWHERE TO BE.
JOE! STOP FOOLING AROUND WITH THOSE THINGS AND LET'S GET OUT OF HERE.
WE NEED TO GET TO THAT APARTMENT BEFORE THOSE KIDS GET BACK.

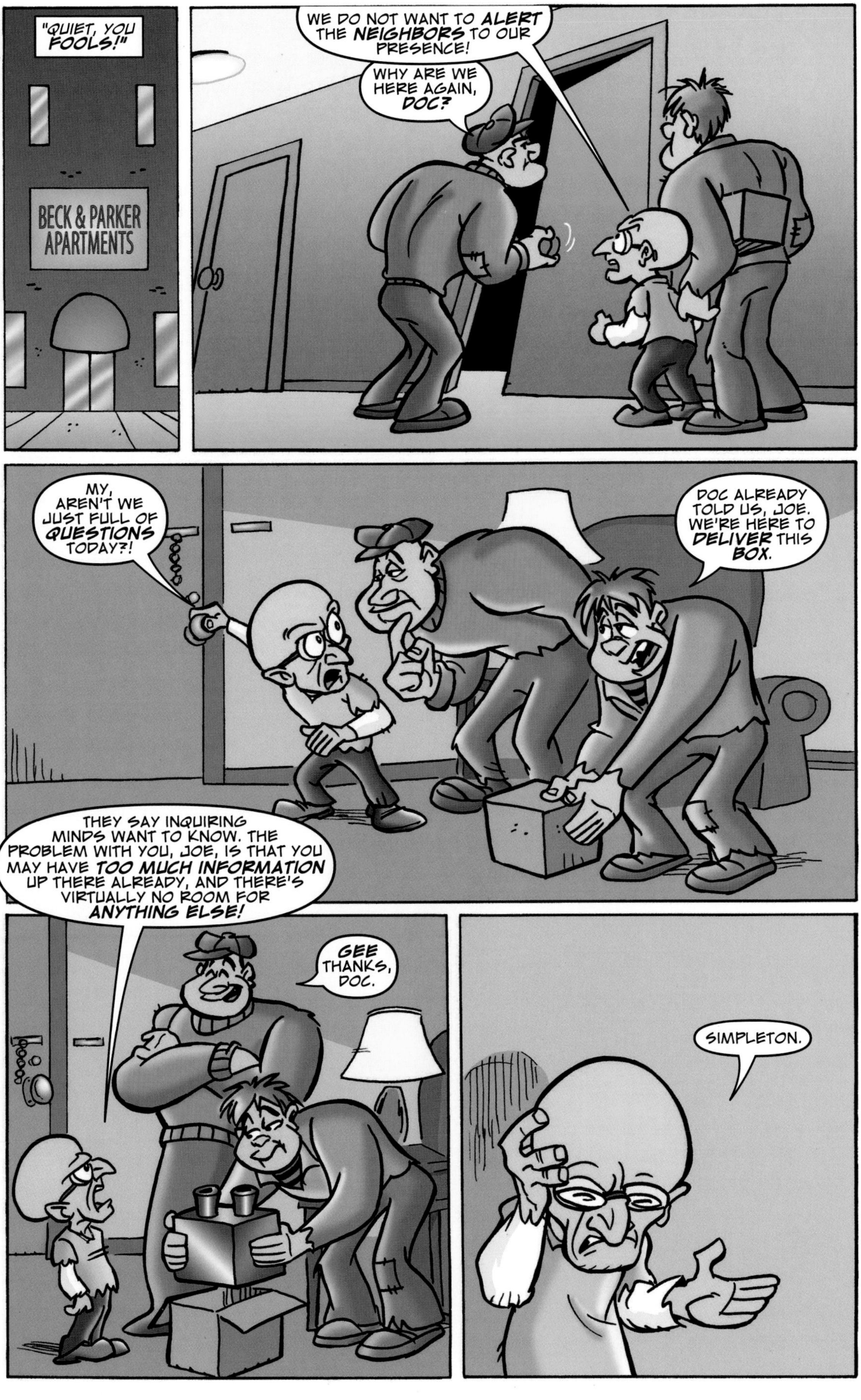
"QUIET, YOU FOOLS!"
BECK & PARKER APARTMENTS
WE DO NOT WANT TO ALERT THE NEIGHBORS TO OUR PRESENCE!
WHY ARE WE HERE AGAIN, DOC?
MY, AREN'T WE JUST FULL OF QUESTIONS TODAY?!
DOC ALREADY TOLD US, JOE. WE'RE HERE TO DELIVER THIS BOX.
THEY SAY INQUIRING MINDS WANT TO KNOW. THE PROBLEM WITH YOU, JOE, IS THAT YOU MAY HAVE TOO MUCH INFORMATION UP THERE ALREADY, AND THERE'S VIRTUALLY NO ROOM FOR ANYTHING ELSE!
GEE THANKS, DOC.
SIMPLETON.

PUT IT UNDER THE DESK AND MAKE SURE IT IS WELL COVERED, SO THEY DON'T SPOT IT.

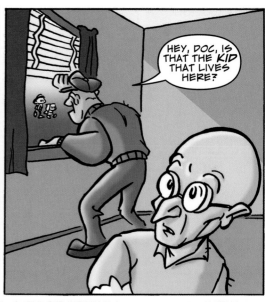

HEY, DOC, IS THAT THE *KID* THAT LIVES HERE?

QUICKLY! BEFORE THEY SPOT US!

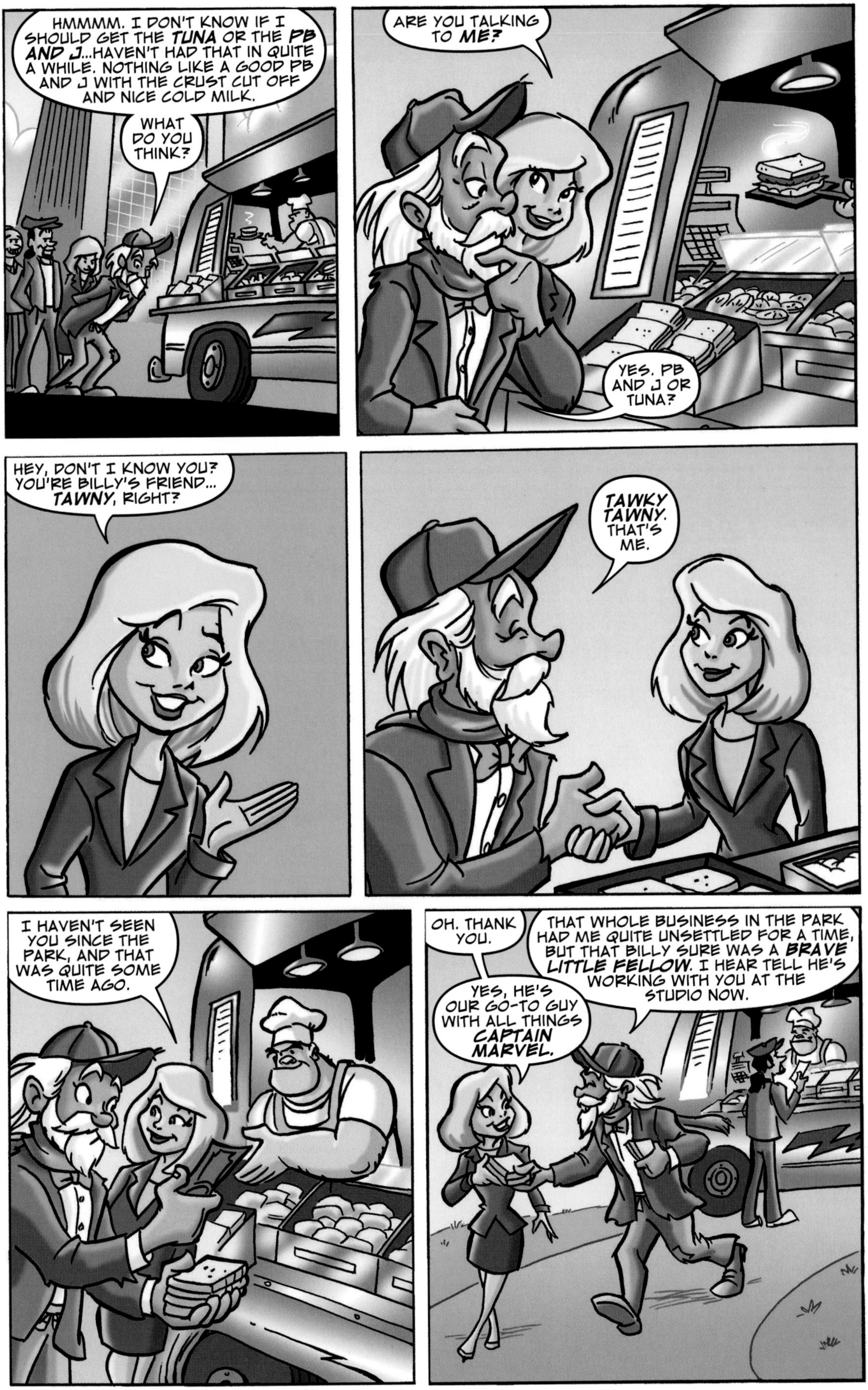
HMMMM. I DON'T KNOW IF I SHOULD GET THE TUNA OR THE PB AND J...HAVEN'T HAD THAT IN QUITE A WHILE. NOTHING LIKE A GOOD PB AND J WITH THE CRUST CUT OFF AND NICE COLD MILK.
WHAT DO YOU THINK?
ARE YOU TALKING TO ME?
YES. PB AND J OR TUNA?
HEY, DON'T I KNOW YOU? YOU'RE BILLY'S FRIEND... TAWNY, RIGHT?
TAWKY TAWNY. THAT'S ME.
I HAVEN'T SEEN YOU SINCE THE PARK, AND THAT WAS QUITE SOME TIME AGO.
OH. THANK YOU.
THAT WHOLE BUSINESS IN THE PARK HAD ME QUITE UNSETTLED FOR A TIME, BUT THAT BILLY SURE WAS A BRAVE LITTLE FELLOW. I HEAR TELL HE'S WORKING WITH YOU AT THE STUDIO NOW.
YES, HE'S OUR GO-TO GUY WITH ALL THINGS CAPTAIN MARVEL.

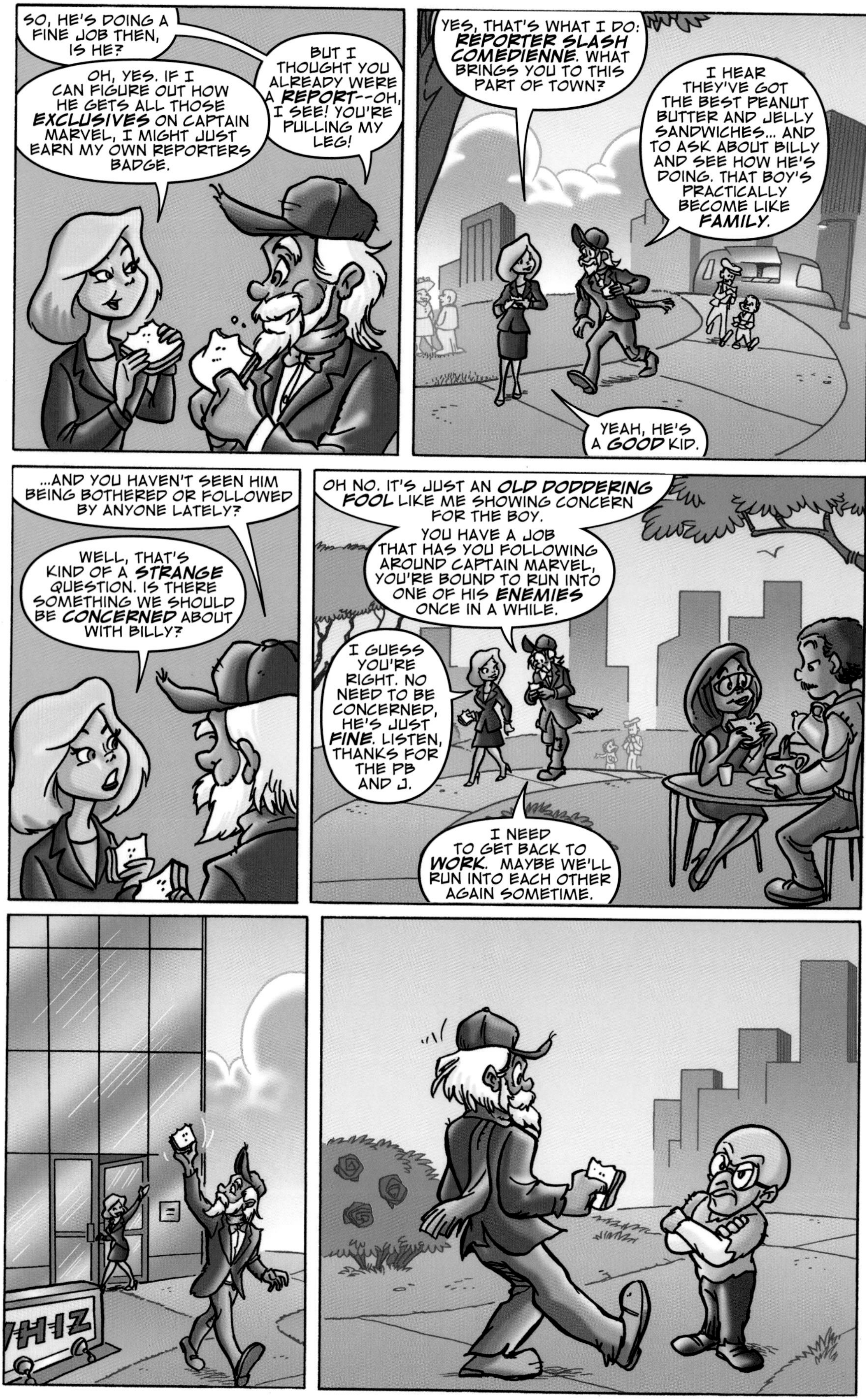

SO, HE'S DOING A FINE JOB THEN, IS HE?
OH, YES. IF I CAN FIGURE OUT HOW HE GETS ALL THOSE EXCLUSIVES ON CAPTAIN MARVEL, I MIGHT JUST EARN MY OWN REPORTERS BADGE.
BUT I THOUGHT YOU ALREADY WERE A REPORT--OH, I SEE! YOU'RE PULLING MY LEG!
YES, THAT'S WHAT I DO: REPORTER SLASH COMEDIENNE. WHAT BRINGS YOU TO THIS PART OF TOWN?
I HEAR THEY'VE GOT THE BEST PEANUT BUTTER AND JELLY SANDWICHES... AND TO ASK ABOUT BILLY AND SEE HOW HE'S DOING. THAT BOY'S PRACTICALLY BECOME LIKE FAMILY.
YEAH, HE'S A GOOD KID.
...AND YOU HAVEN'T SEEN HIM BEING BOTHERED OR FOLLOWED BY ANYONE LATELY?
WELL, THAT'S KIND OF A STRANGE QUESTION. IS THERE SOMETHING WE SHOULD BE CONCERNED ABOUT WITH BILLY?
OH NO. IT'S JUST AN OLD DODDERING FOOL LIKE ME SHOWING CONCERN FOR THE BOY.
YOU HAVE A JOB THAT HAS YOU FOLLOWING AROUND CAPTAIN MARVEL, YOU'RE BOUND TO RUN INTO ONE OF HIS ENEMIES ONCE IN A WHILE.
I GUESS YOU'RE RIGHT. NO NEED TO BE CONCERNED, HE'S JUST FINE. LISTEN, THANKS FOR THE PB AND J.
I NEED TO GET BACK TO WORK. MAYBE WE'LL RUN INTO EACH OTHER AGAIN SOMETIME.
WHIZ

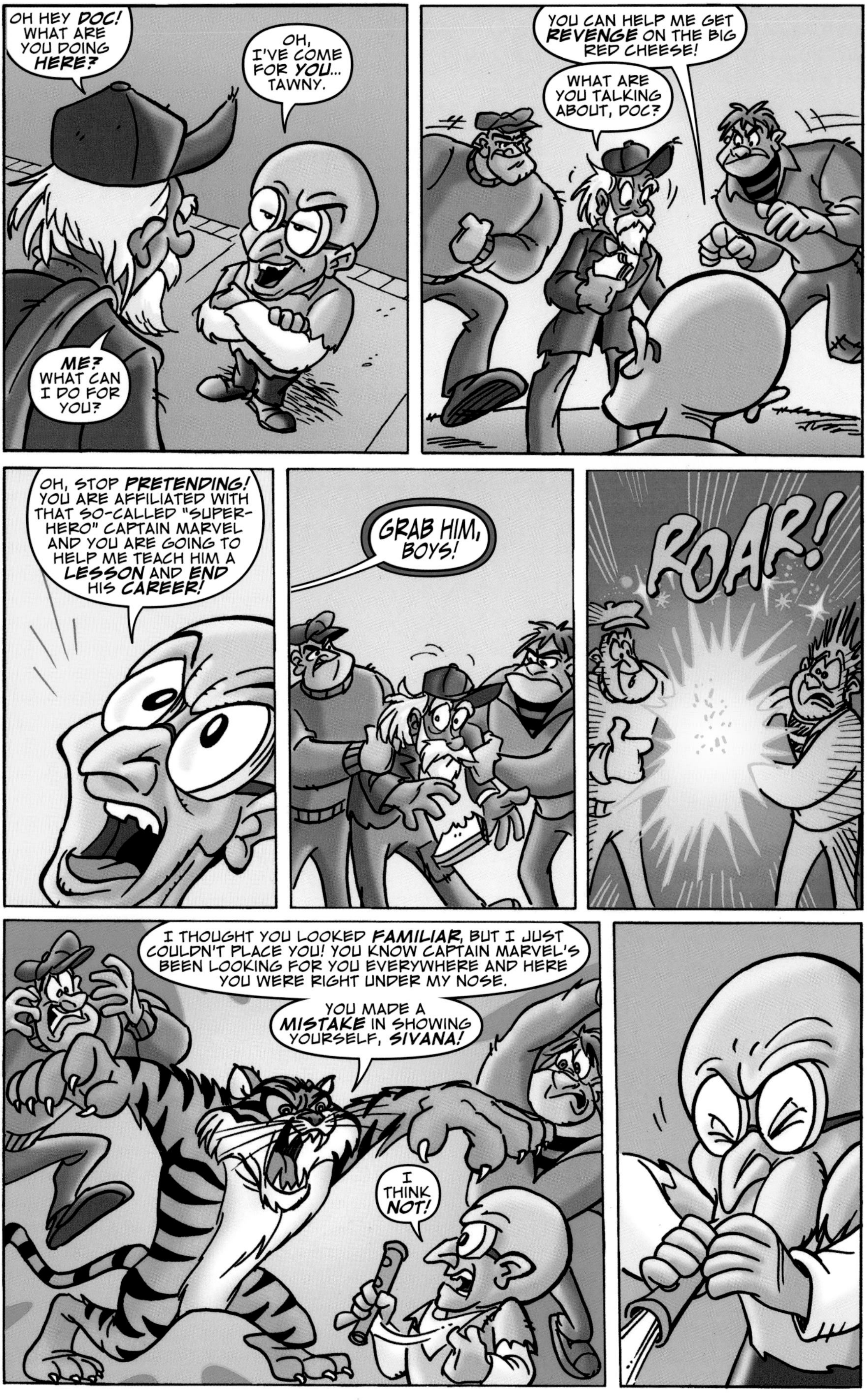
OH HEY DOC! WHAT ARE YOU DOING HERE?
OH, I'VE COME FOR YOU... TAWNY.
ME? WHAT CAN I DO FOR YOU?
YOU CAN HELP ME GET REVENGE ON THE BIG RED CHEESE!
WHAT ARE YOU TALKING ABOUT, DOC?
OH, STOP PRETENDING! YOU ARE AFFILIATED WITH THAT SO-CALLED "SUPER-HERO" CAPTAIN MARVEL AND YOU ARE GOING TO HELP ME TEACH HIM A LESSON AND END HIS CAREER!
GRAB HIM, BOYS!
ROAR!
I THOUGHT YOU LOOKED FAMILIAR, BUT I JUST COULDN'T PLACE YOU! YOU KNOW CAPTAIN MARVEL'S BEEN LOOKING FOR YOU EVERYWHERE AND HERE YOU WERE RIGHT UNDER MY NOSE.
YOU MADE A MISTAKE IN SHOWING YOURSELF, SIVANA!
I THINK NOT!

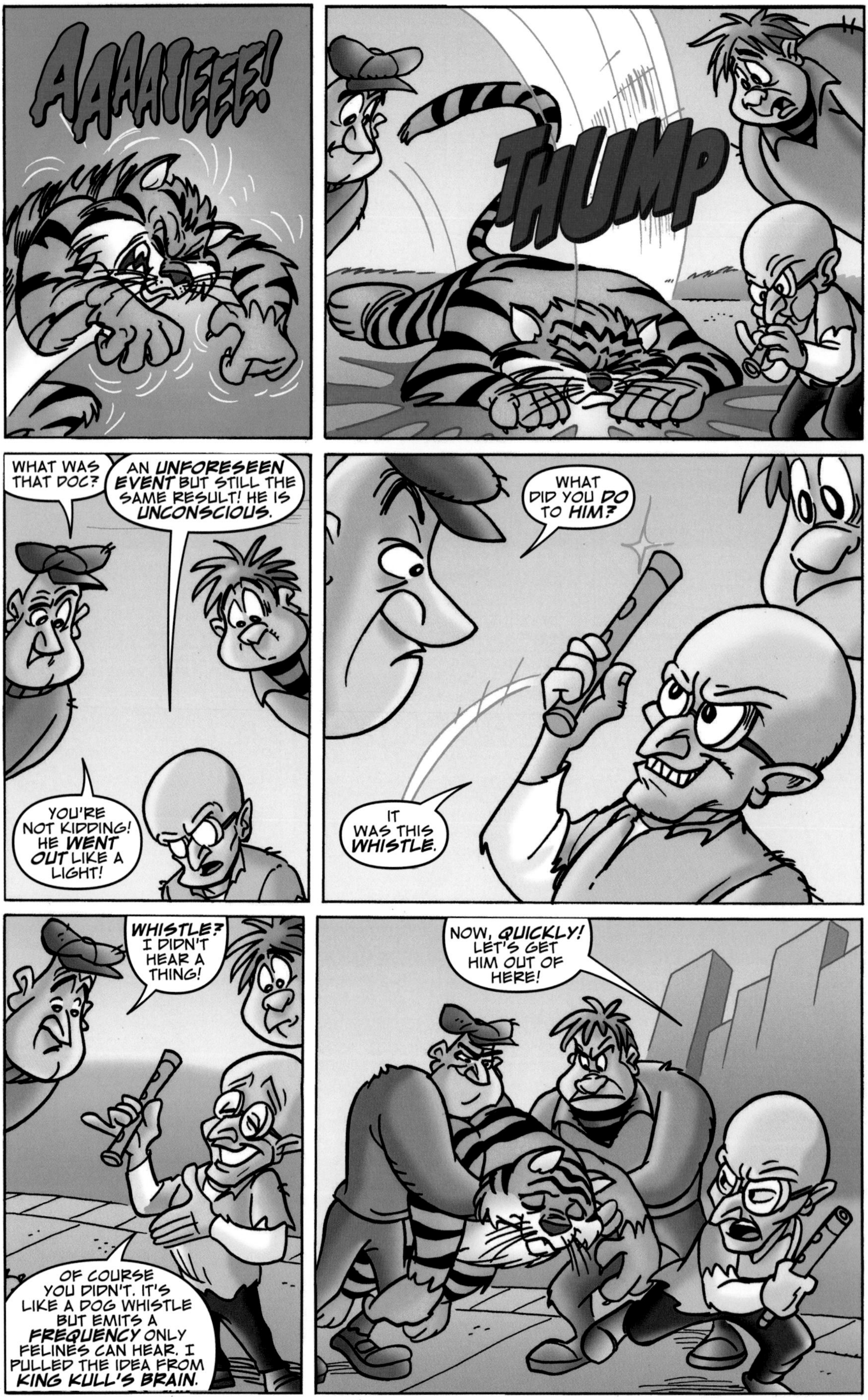
AAAAIEEE!
THUMP
WHAT WAS THAT DOC?
AN UNFORESEEN EVENT BUT STILL THE SAME RESULT! HE IS UNCONSCIOUS.
YOU'RE NOT KIDDING! HE WENT OUT LIKE A LIGHT!
WHAT DID YOU DO TO HIM?
IT WAS THIS WHISTLE.
WHISTLE? I DIDN'T HEAR A THING!
OF COURSE YOU DIDN'T. IT'S LIKE A DOG WHISTLE BUT EMITS A FREQUENCY ONLY FELINES CAN HEAR. I PULLED THE IDEA FROM KING KULL'S BRAIN.
NOW, QUICKLY! LET'S GET HIM OUT OF HERE!

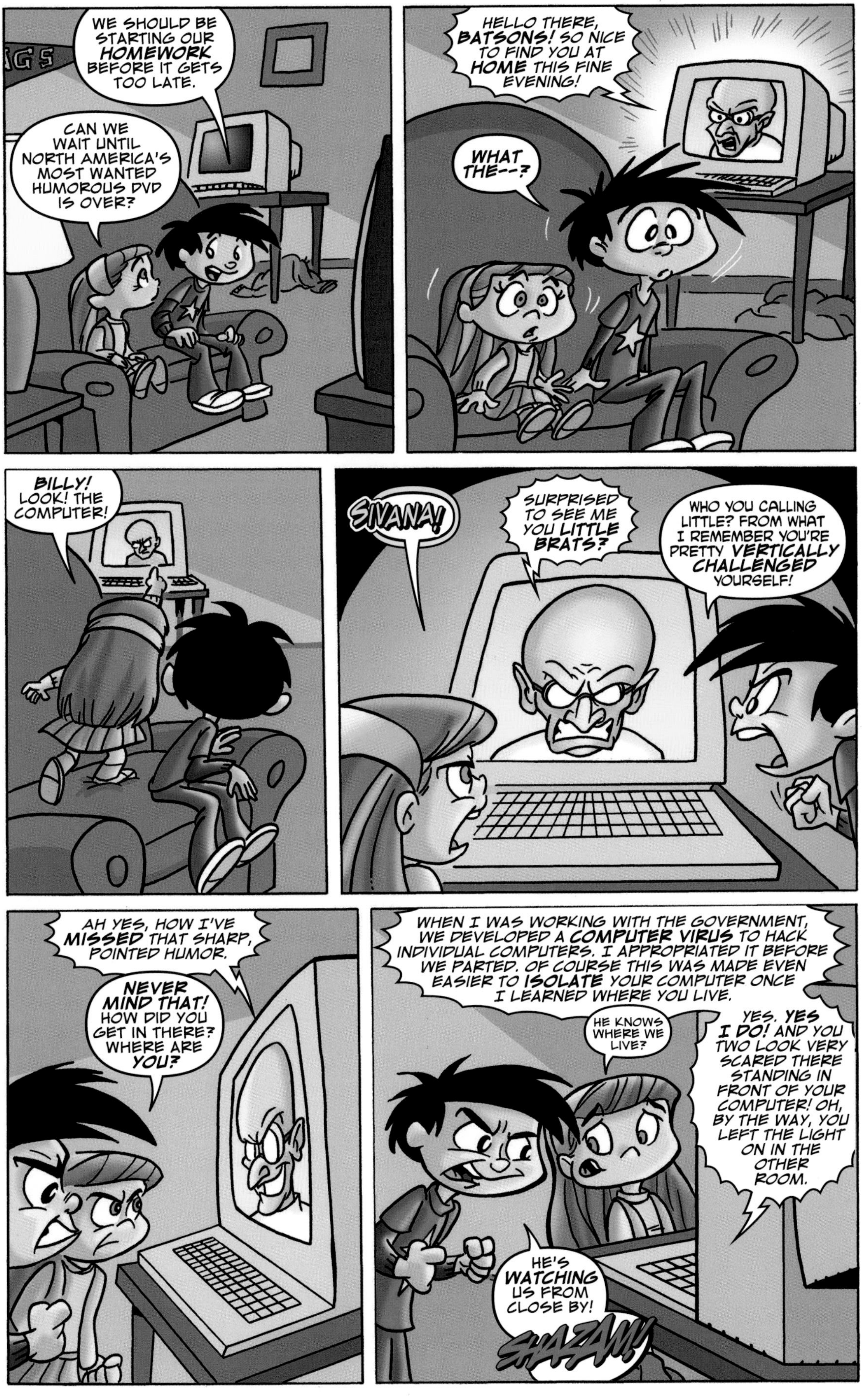

WE SHOULD BE STARTING OUR HOMEWORK BEFORE IT GETS TOO LATE.
CAN WE WAIT UNTIL NORTH AMERICA'S MOST WANTED HUMOROUS DVD IS OVER?
HELLO THERE, BATSONS! SO NICE TO FIND YOU AT HOME THIS FINE EVENING!
WHAT THE--?
BILLY! LOOK! THE COMPUTER!
SIVANA!
SURPRISED TO SEE ME YOU LITTLE BRATS?
WHO YOU CALLING LITTLE? FROM WHAT I REMEMBER YOU'RE PRETTY VERTICALLY CHALLENGED YOURSELF!
AH YES, HOW I'VE MISSED THAT SHARP, POINTED HUMOR.
NEVER MIND THAT! HOW DID YOU GET IN THERE? WHERE ARE YOU?
WHEN I WAS WORKING WITH THE GOVERNMENT, WE DEVELOPED A COMPUTER VIRUS TO HACK INDIVIDUAL COMPUTERS. I APPROPRIATED IT BEFORE WE PARTED. OF COURSE THIS WAS MADE EVEN EASIER TO ISOLATE YOUR COMPUTER ONCE I LEARNED WHERE YOU LIVE.
HE KNOWS WHERE WE LIVE?
YES. YES I DO! AND YOU TWO LOOK VERY SCARED THERE STANDING IN FRONT OF YOUR COMPUTER! OH, BY THE WAY, YOU LEFT THE LIGHT ON IN THE OTHER ROOM.
HE'S WATCHING US FROM CLOSE BY!
SHAZAM!

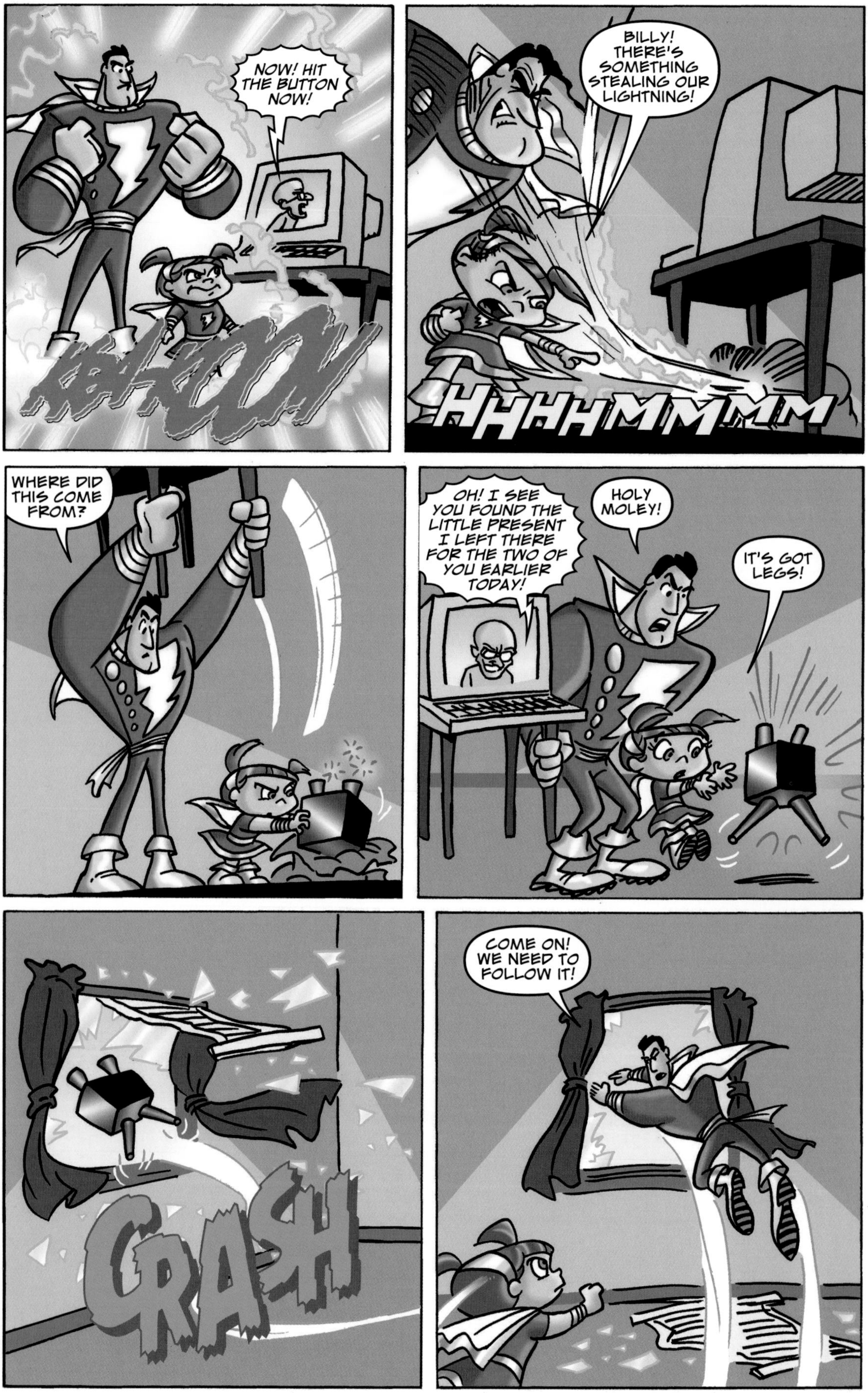
NOW! HIT THE BUTTON NOW!
KRAKOOM
BILLY! THERE'S SOMETHING STEALING OUR LIGHTNING!
HHHHMMMMM
WHERE DID THIS COME FROM?
OH! I SEE YOU FOUND THE LITTLE PRESENT I LEFT THERE FOR THE TWO OF YOU EARLIER TODAY!
HOLY MOLEY!
IT'S GOT LEGS!
CRASH
COME ON! WE NEED TO FOLLOW IT!

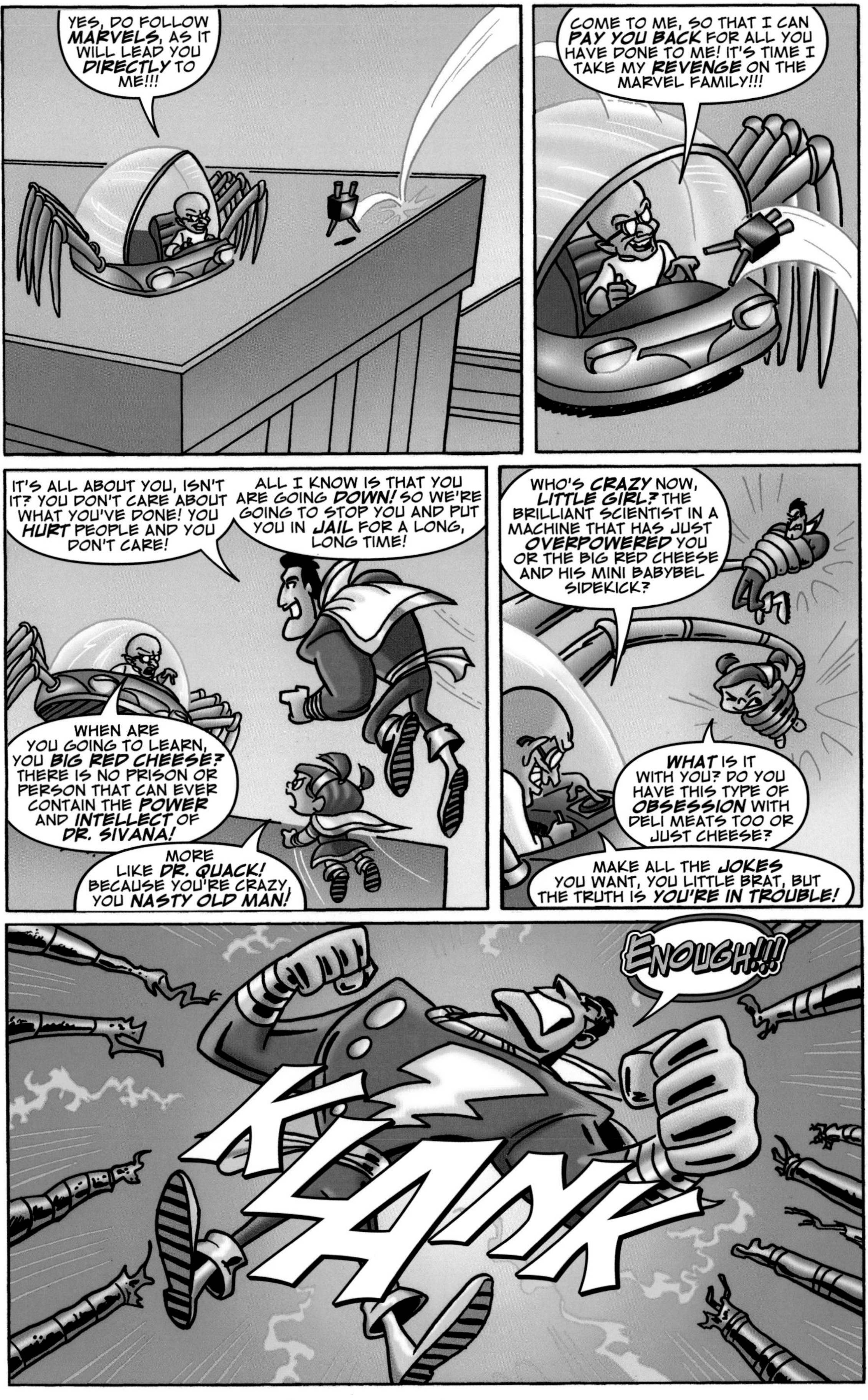
YES, DO FOLLOW MARVELS, AS IT WILL LEAD YOU DIRECTLY TO ME!!!
COME TO ME, SO THAT I CAN PAY YOU BACK FOR ALL YOU HAVE DONE TO ME! IT'S TIME I TAKE MY REVENGE ON THE MARVEL FAMILY!!!
IT'S ALL ABOUT YOU, ISN'T IT? YOU DON'T CARE ABOUT WHAT YOU'VE DONE! YOU HURT PEOPLE AND YOU DON'T CARE!
ALL I KNOW IS THAT YOU ARE GOING DOWN! SO WE'RE GOING TO STOP YOU AND PUT YOU IN JAIL FOR A LONG, LONG TIME!
WHEN ARE YOU GOING TO LEARN, YOU BIG RED CHEESE? THERE IS NO PRISON OR PERSON THAT CAN EVER CONTAIN THE POWER AND INTELLECT OF DR. SIVANA!
MORE LIKE DR. QUACK! BECAUSE YOU'RE CRAZY, YOU NASTY OLD MAN!
WHO'S CRAZY NOW, LITTLE GIRL? THE BRILLIANT SCIENTIST IN A MACHINE THAT HAS JUST OVERPOWERED YOU OR THE BIG RED CHEESE AND HIS MINI BABYBEL SIDEKICK?
WHAT IS IT WITH YOU? DO YOU HAVE THIS TYPE OF OBSESSION WITH DELI MEATS TOO OR JUST CHEESE?
MAKE ALL THE JOKES YOU WANT, YOU LITTLE BRAT, BUT THE TRUTH IS YOU'RE IN TROUBLE!
ENOUGH!!!
KLANK

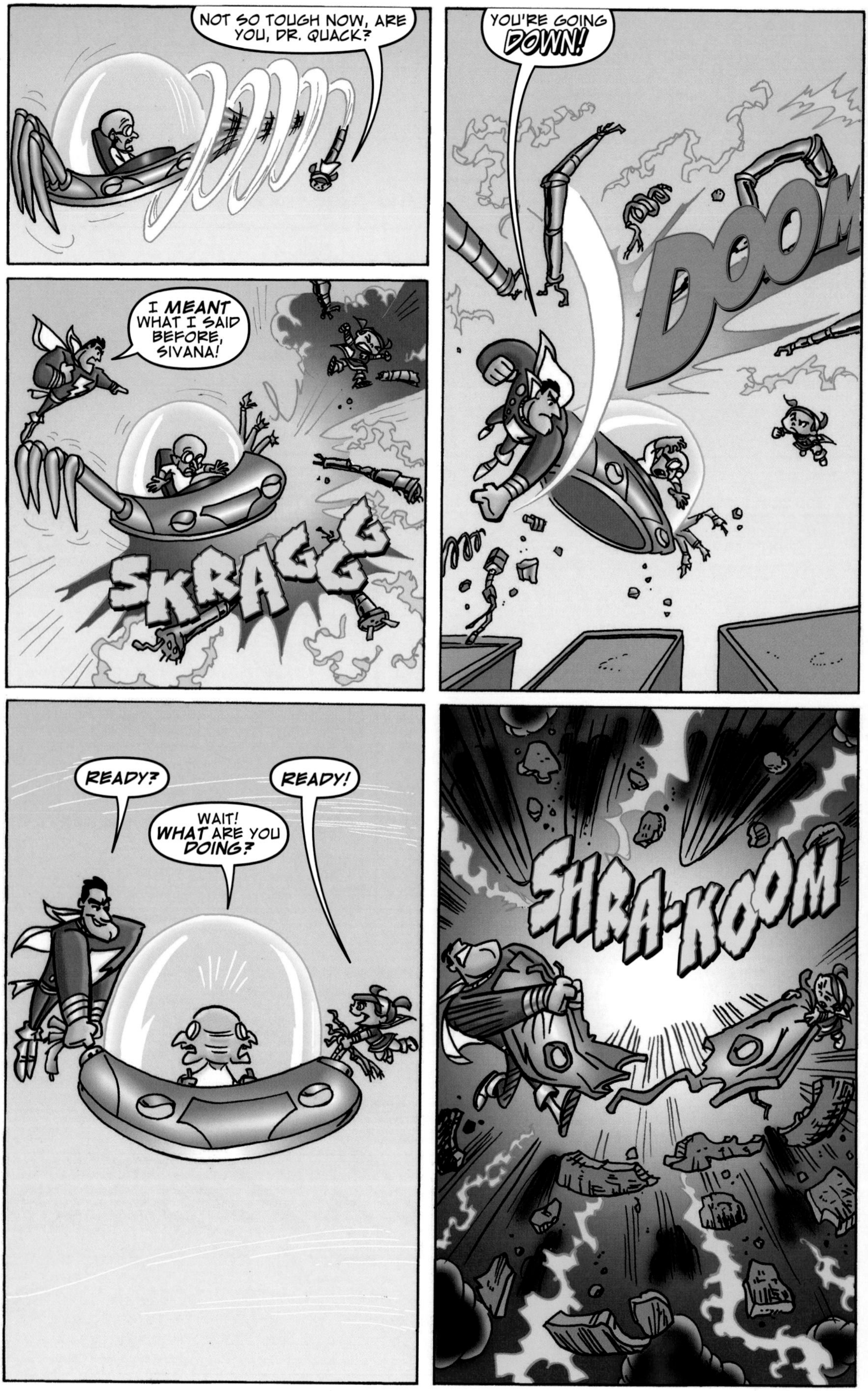
NOT SO TOUGH NOW, ARE YOU, DR. QUACK?
YOU'RE GOING DOWN!
DOOM
I MEANT WHAT I SAID BEFORE, SIVANA!
SKRAGG
READY?
WAIT! WHAT ARE YOU DOING?
READY!
SHRA-KOOM

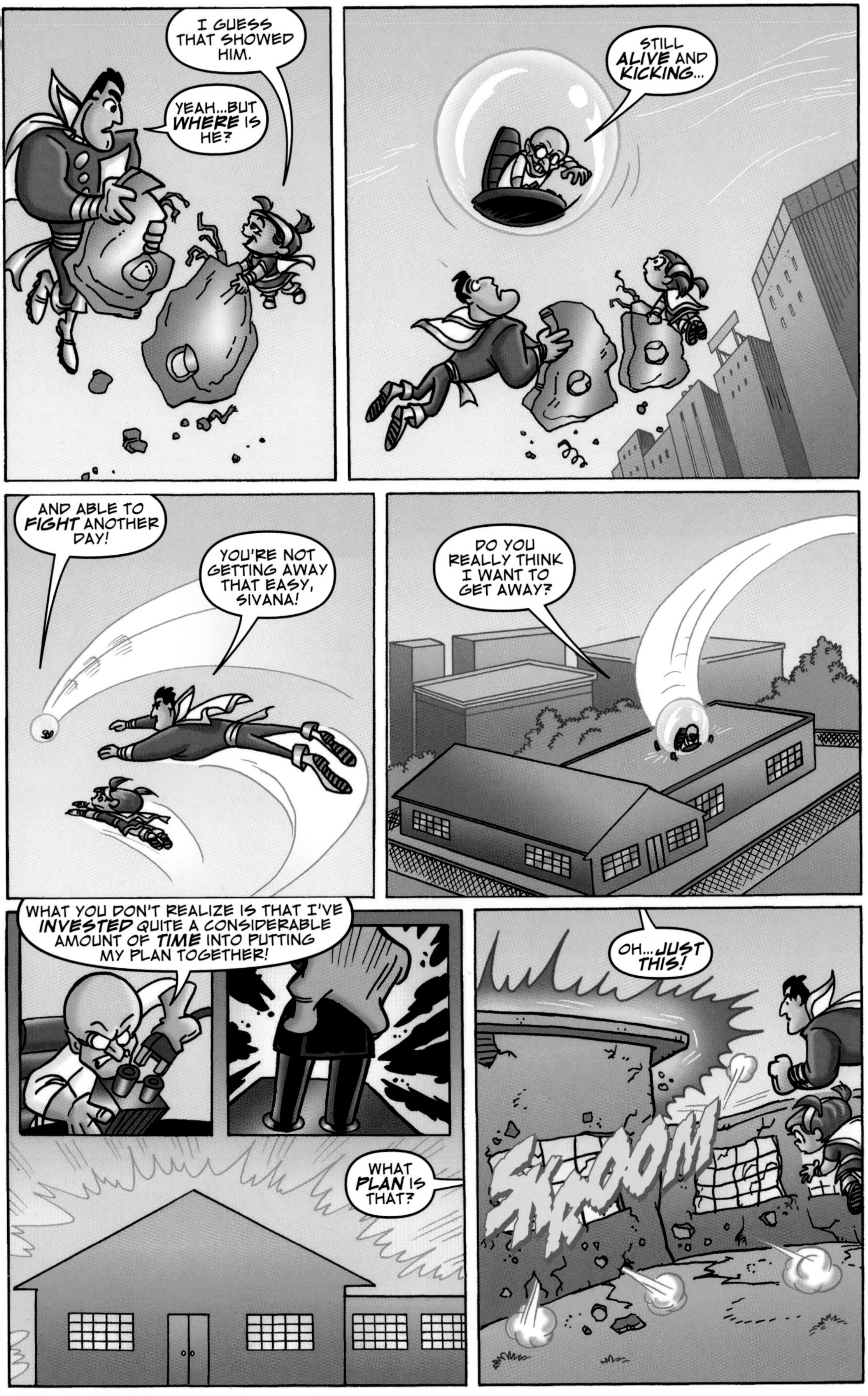
I GUESS THAT SHOWED HIM.
YEAH...BUT WHERE IS HE?
STILL ALIVE AND KICKING...
AND ABLE TO FIGHT ANOTHER DAY!
YOU'RE NOT GETTING AWAY THAT EASY, SIVANA!
DO YOU REALLY THINK I WANT TO GET AWAY?
WHAT YOU DON'T REALIZE IS THAT I'VE INVESTED QUITE A CONSIDERABLE AMOUNT OF TIME INTO PUTTING MY PLAN TOGETHER!
WHAT PLAN IS THAT?
OH...JUST THIS!
SKOOM

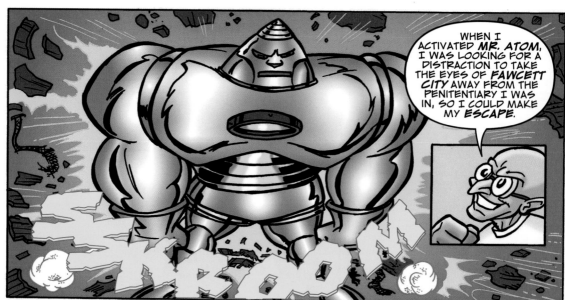

WHEN I ACTIVATED **MR. ATOM**, I WAS LOOKING FOR A DISTRACTION TO TAKE THE EYES OF **FAWCETT CITY** AWAY FROM THE PENITENTIARY I WAS IN, SO I COULD MAKE MY **ESCAPE.**

THANKS TO YOU, "BILLY," FOR **FIGHTING** HIM IN FRONT OF ALL THOSE CAMERAS.

...BUT YOU SEEMED TO HAVE A BIT OF A **TOUGH TIME** WITH HIM.

DON'T WORRY! I'LL DO THE SAME THING TO THIS ONE!

WE WILL!

AH AH AH! THIS ONE IS GOING TO BE REALLY **TOUGH** TO **DEFEAT.** YES, HE'S BIGGER AND I THINK YOU WOULD EVENTUALLY FIND A WAY TO **DESTROY** IT, TOO...

...BUT I'VE TAKEN **PRECAUTIONS** TO ENSURE THAT WON'T HAPPEN!

TEK

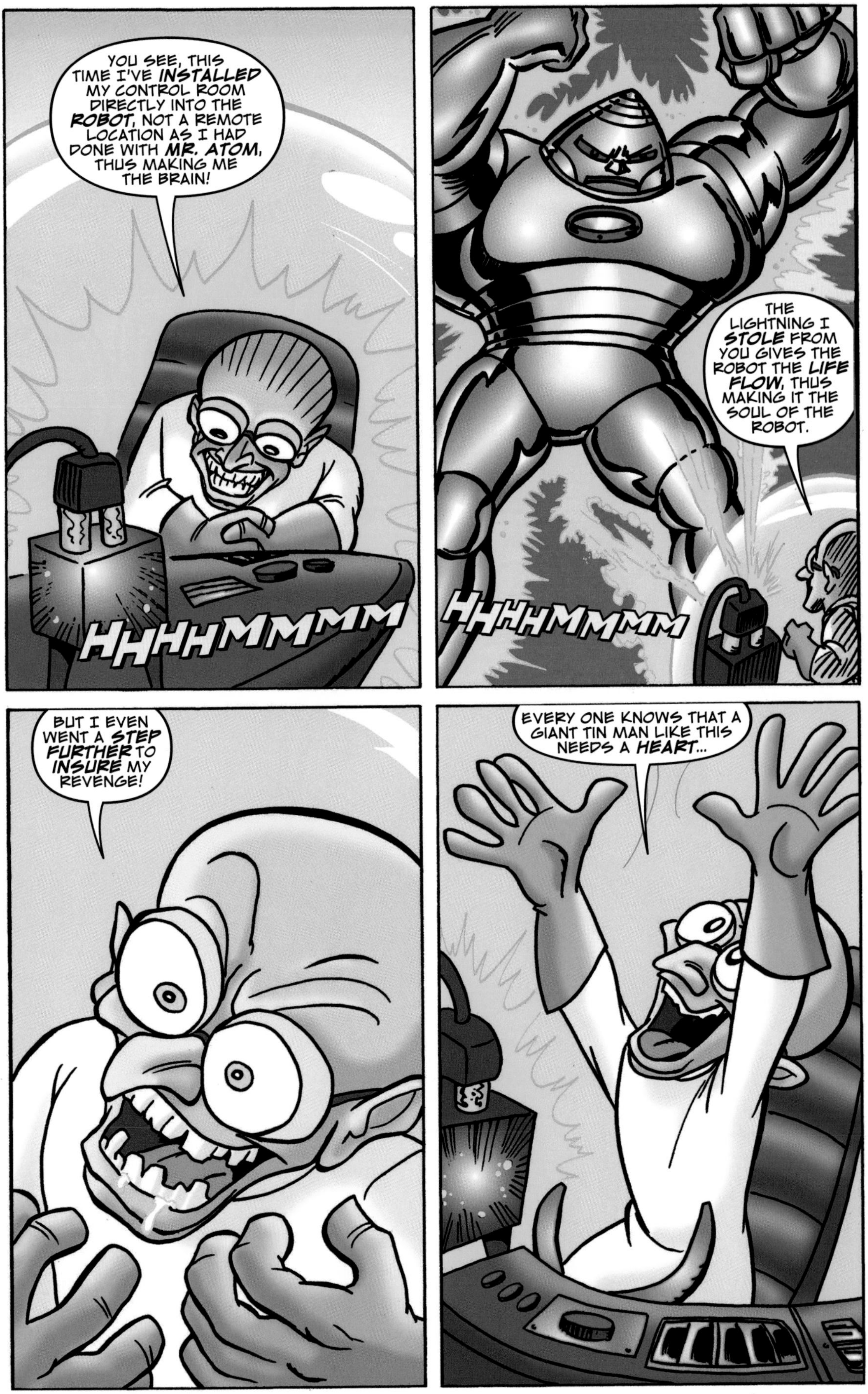

YOU SEE, THIS TIME I'VE INSTALLED MY CONTROL ROOM DIRECTLY INTO THE ROBOT, NOT A REMOTE LOCATION AS I HAD DONE WITH MR. ATOM, THUS MAKING ME THE BRAIN!
HHHHMMMMM
THE LIGHTNING I STOLE FROM YOU GIVES THE ROBOT THE LIFE FLOW, THUS MAKING IT THE SOUL OF THE ROBOT.
HHHHMMMMM
BUT I EVEN WENT A STEP FURTHER TO INSURE MY REVENGE!
EVERY ONE KNOWS THAT A GIANT TIN MAN LIKE THIS NEEDS A HEART...

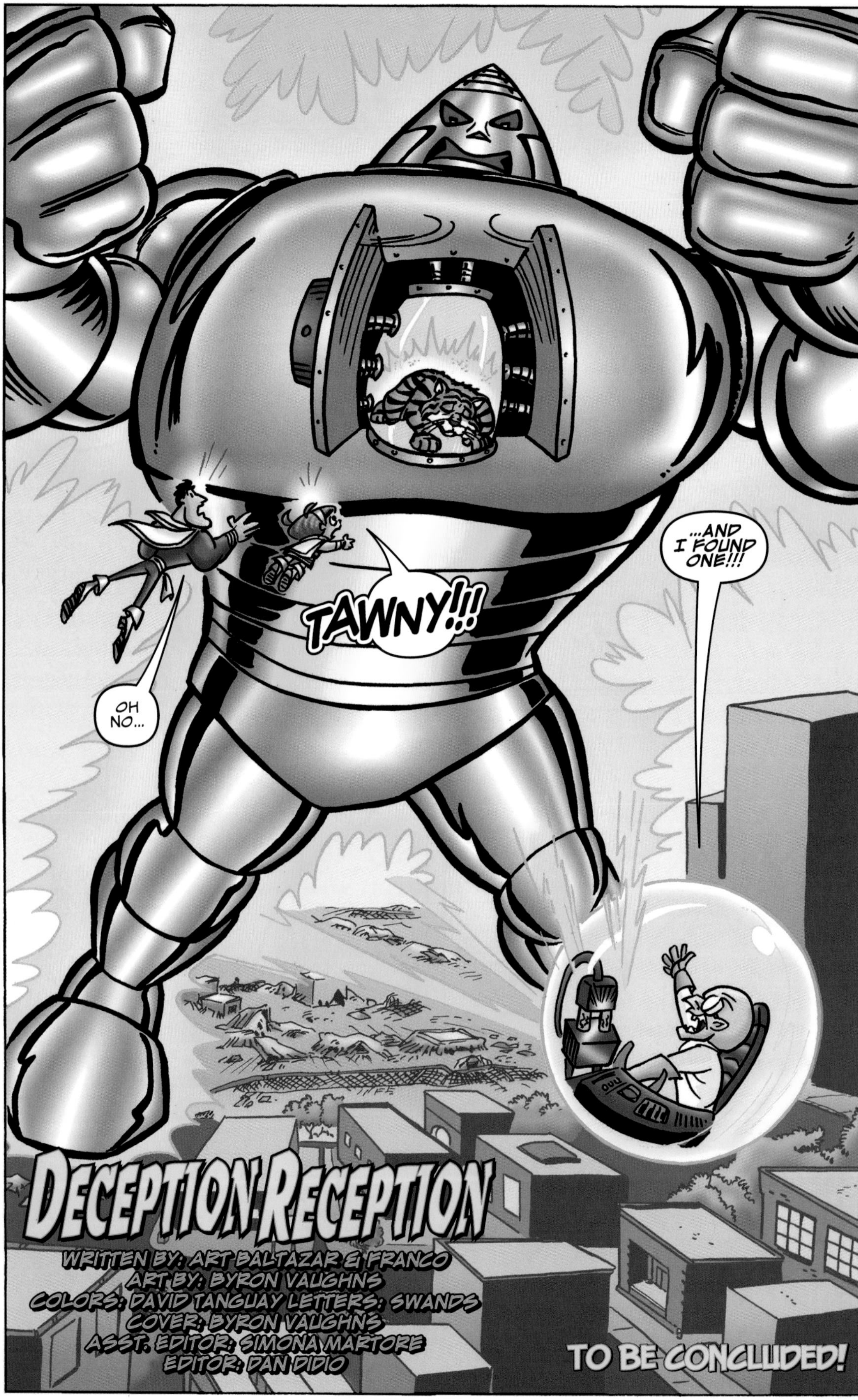
TAWNY!!!
OH NO...
...AND I FOUND ONE!!!
DECEPTION RECEPTION
WRITTEN BY: ART BALTAZAR & FRANCO
ART BY: BYRON VAUGHNS
COLORS: DAVID TANGUAY LETTERS: SWANDS
COVER: BYRON VAUGHNS
ASST. EDITOR: SIMONA MARTORE
EDITOR: DAN DIDIO
TO BE CONCLUDED!

CREATORS

ART BALTAZAR - CO-WRITER

Born in Chicago, **Art Baltazar** has been cartooning ever since he can recall. Art has worked on award-winning series like Tiny Titans and Superman Family Adventures. He lives outside of Chicago with his wife, Rose, and children Sonny, Gordon, and Audrey.

FRANCO - CO-WRITER

Franco Aureliani has been drawing comics ever since he could hold a crayon. He resides in upstate New York with his wife, Ivette, and son, Nicolas, and spends most of his days working on comics. Franco has worked on Superman Family Adventures and Tiny Titans, and he also teaches high school art.

GLOSSARY

affiliated (uh-FILL-ee-ay-tid)--closely connected with something or someone

alter ego (AHL-ter EE-goh)--a different version of yourself that is often secret

comedienne (kom-ee-dee-EHN)--a female comedian or actress

coot (KOOT)--a strange and usually old man

culprit (KUHL-prit)--a person who has committed a crime or done something wrong

dispel (di-SPELL)--to make something (such as a belief, feeling, idea, or magic spell) go away or end

doddering (DOD-er-ing)--walking and moving in a slow and unsteady way because of old age

frequency (FREE-kwuhn-see)--the number of times that something (such as a sound wave or radio wave) is repeated in a period of time

isolate (AY-soh-layt)--to put or keep (someone or something) in a place or situation that is separate

malevolence (muh-LEV-uh-luhnss)--having or showing a desire to cause harm to another person

precautions (pri-KAW-shuhnz)--things that are done to prevent possible harm or trouble from happening

unanimated (uhn-AN-nuh-may-tid)--devoid of life and energy

vagrant (VAY-gruhnt)--a person who has no place to live and no job and who asks people for money

VISUAL QUESTIONS & PROMPTS

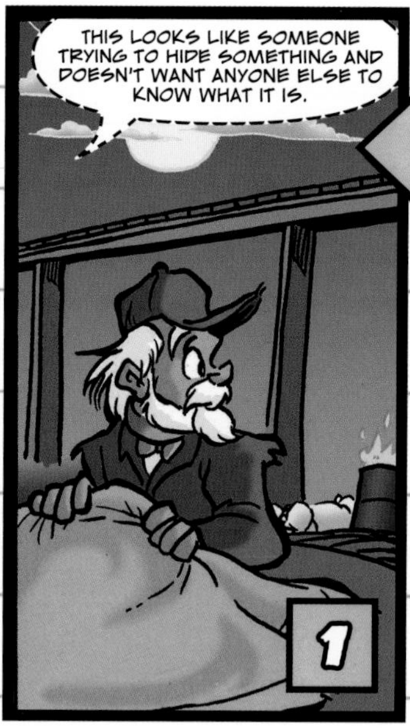

THIS LOOKS LIKE SOMEONE TRYING TO HIDE SOMETHING AND DOESN'T WANT ANYONE ELSE TO KNOW WHAT IT IS.
1

1. Why is there a dotted line around this speech bubble?

2. What is happening in this panel? Explain it in your own words. What are some other ways this action could've been shown?

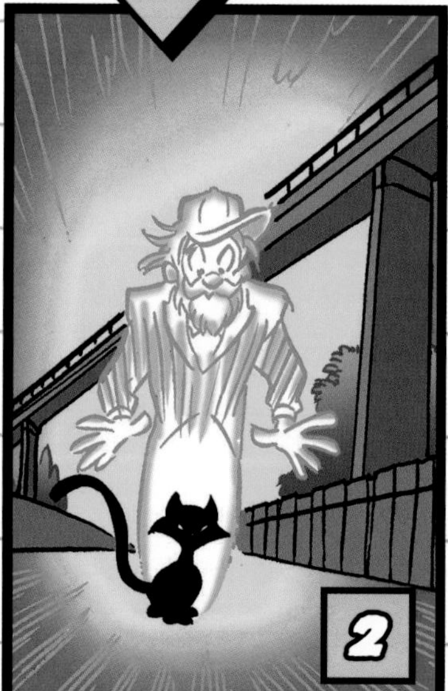

2

3. This word bubble looks different than the rest. Why is it different? What does it mean?

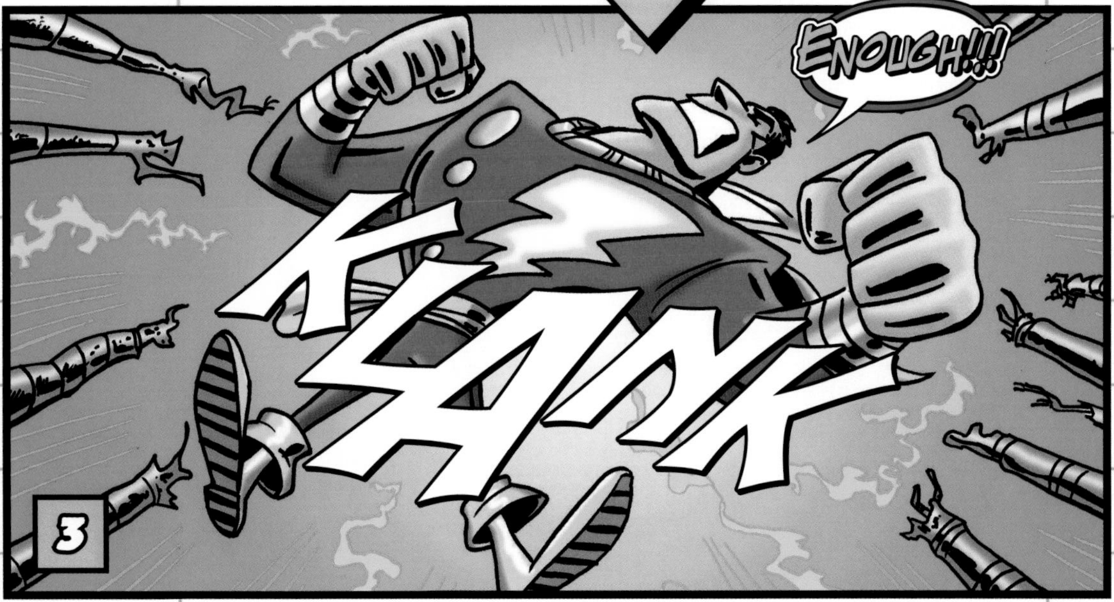
ENOUGH!!!
KLANK
3

4. Why is Dr. Sivana pretending to be homeless?

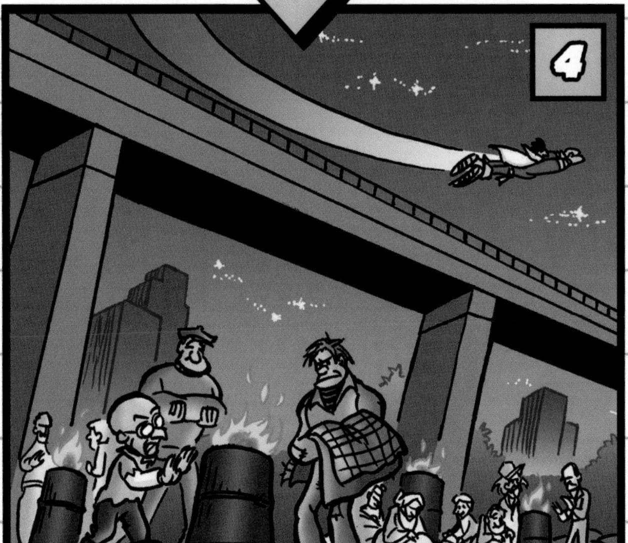
4

READ THEM ALL!

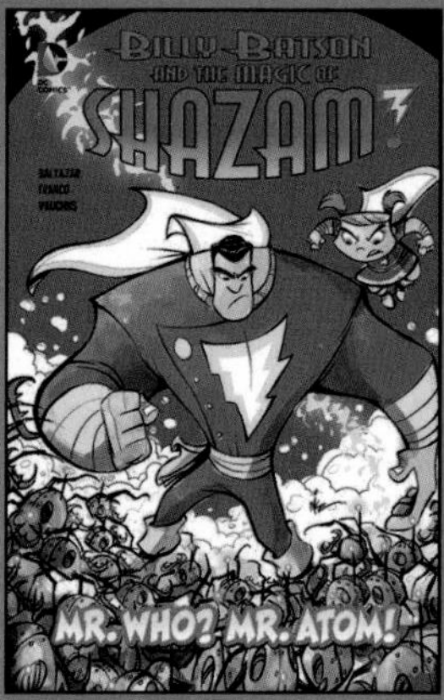
BILLY BATSON AND THE MAGIC OF SHAZAM!
BALTAZAR
FRANCO
VAUGHNS
MR. WHO? MR. ATOM!

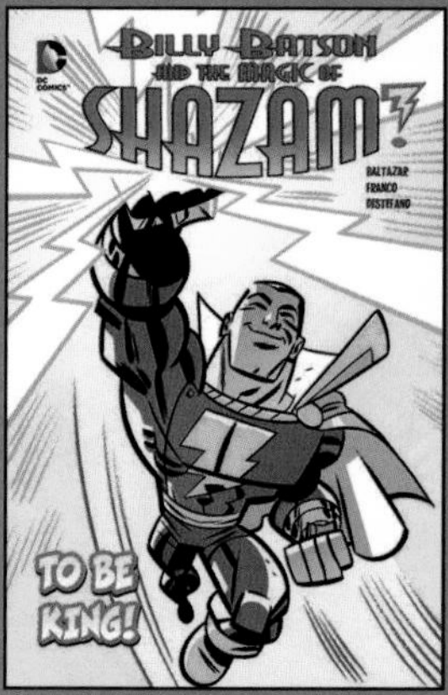
BILLY BATSON AND THE MAGIC OF SHAZAM!
BALTAZAR
FRANCO
DISTEFANO
TO BE KING!

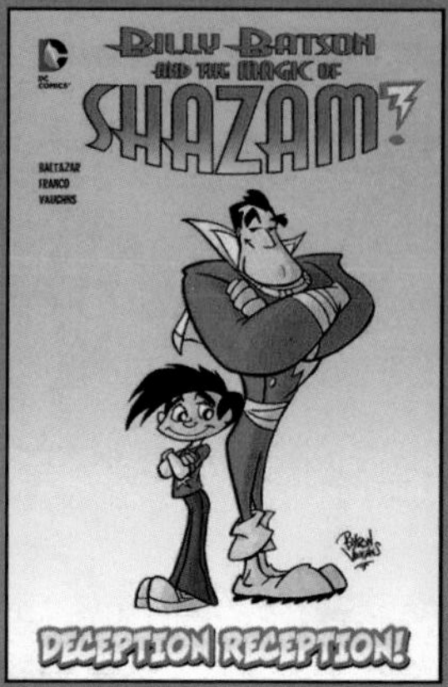
BILLY BATSON AND THE MAGIC OF SHAZAM!
BALTAZAR
FRANCO
VAUGHNS
DECEPTION RECEPTION!

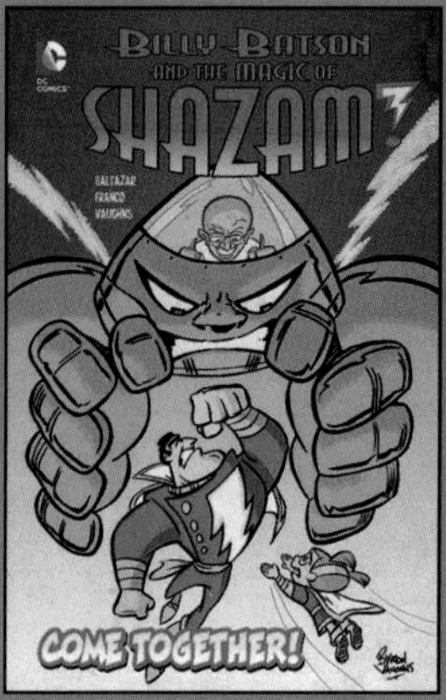
BILLY BATSON AND THE MAGIC OF SHAZAM!
BALTAZAR
FRANCO
VAUGHNS
COME TOGETHER!

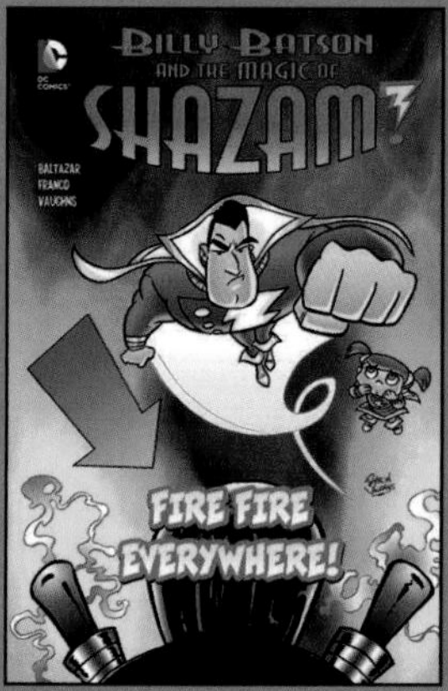
BILLY BATSON AND THE MAGIC OF SHAZAM!
BALTAZAR
FRANCO
VAUGHNS
FIRE FIRE EVERYWHERE!

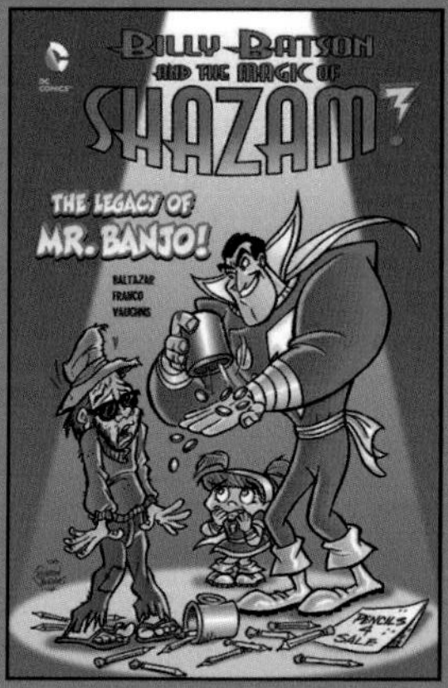
BILLY BATSON AND THE MAGIC OF SHAZAM!
THE LEGACY OF MR. BANJO!
BALTAZAR
FRANCO
VAUGHNS

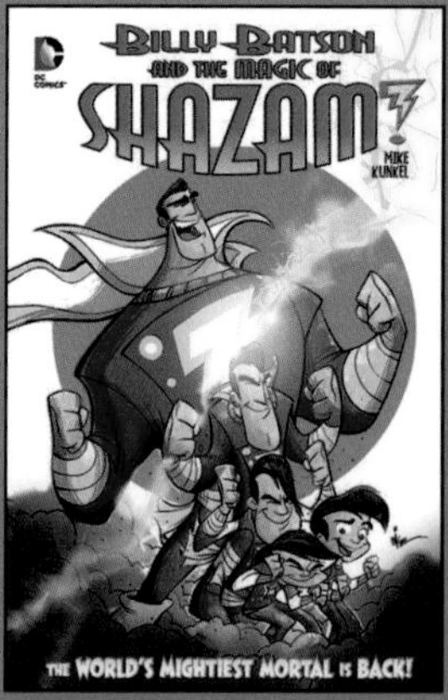
BILLY BATSON AND THE MAGIC OF SHAZAM!
MIKE KUNKEL
THE WORLD'S MIGHTIEST MORTAL IS BACK!

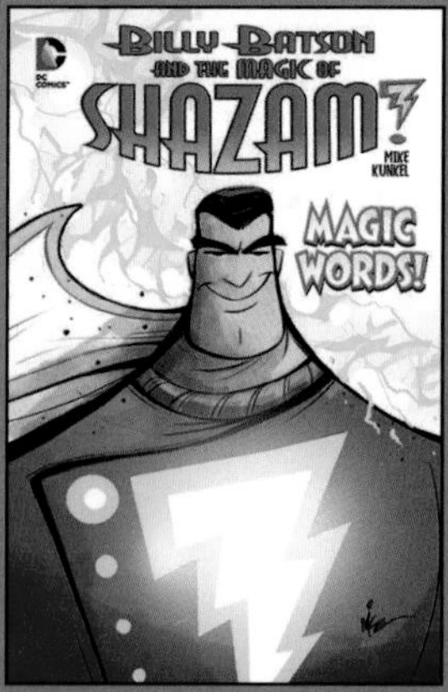
BILLY BATSON AND THE MAGIC OF SHAZAM!
MIKE KUNKEL
MAGIC WORDS!

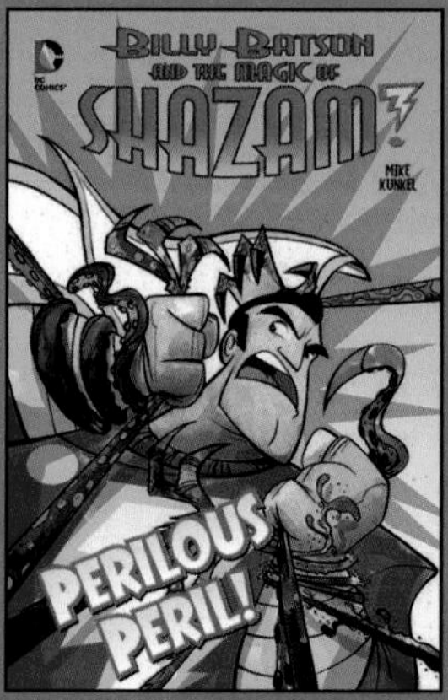
BILLY BATSON AND THE MAGIC OF SHAZAM!
MIKE KUNKEL
PERILOUS PERIL!

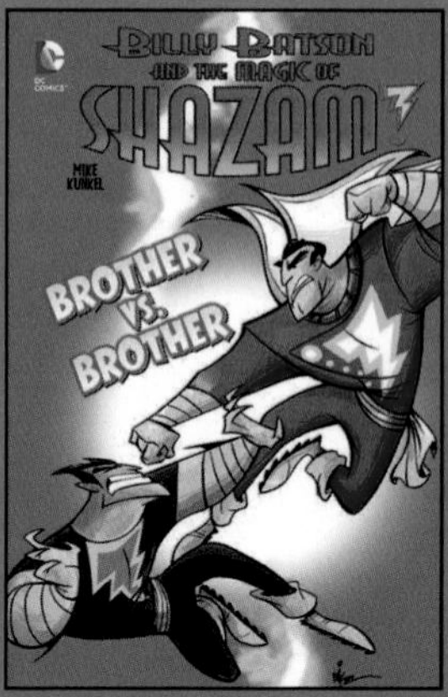
BILLY BATSON AND THE MAGIC OF SHAZAM!
MIKE KUNKEL
BROTHER VS. BROTHER